# Dead Children's Playground

Gulf Coast Paranormal Season Three

Book Three

By M. L. Bullock

# Prologue—1902

*Old Huntsville, Alabama*

The old park in Huntsville, Alabama, always seemed a bit eerie but on this sunny afternoon, it felt like the perfect place to play. The tall, ancient oaks with their Spanish moss looked like they were straight out of a fairy tale. They cast long, twisting shadows over the playground, and the air smelled like decaying leaves mixed with the buzzing of cicadas. It was hot but not too hot.

Cherry was running around with her friends, her short blonde curls bouncing with every step. Her blue eyes sparkled with excitement, and she couldn't stop smiling, even though she had a gap where her front tooth used to be. Her left sock rolled down into her shoe but she kept running.

For just a few moments, she forgot about the missing tooth. The obvious gap really bothered her even though Mommy said it was natural. Cherry accidentally knocked it out when she took a tumble learning to jump rope. But it had been loose anyway.

Today, they were playing tag, and Cherry was "it."

She giggled as she chased her friends around the swings and slide, her dress fluttering around her. Cherry felt so happy, almost like she was flying. The other kids were laughing and shouting too, their voices mixing with the sounds of the park.

For a while, it felt like everything was perfect. Yes, it had been a perfect day.

But even with all their laughter, there was something strange about the park that day. Cherry dragged her feet on the ground, her sock rolling further into her shoe as she slowed down her swinging. She got off the swing and stood staring at the trees behind them. She felt like someone was watching her, but who?

She could not see anyone at all, though the shadows seemed darker and longer, stretching out like they were trying to reach the children.

The stillness at the edges of the park made her shiver, like the trees were watching them play.

*No, that's not right.*

Cherry shook off the feeling and kept running, determined to catch up with her friends.

As she chased her friends, something caught her eye.

Out of the corner of her vision, Cherry saw a shadow move where no shadow should be. she stopped abruptly, her heart pounding, and stared into the darkness under the trees. She blinked and raised her hand to shield her eyes from the fading sunlight.

"Cherry, come on!" one of her friends shouted, breaking her trance. She shook her head and laughed, but the feeling lingered. She had weird goose pimples traveling up and down her body.

The children decided to switch games and started a game of hide-and-seek. Cherry found a great hiding spot behind a big oak tree, its roots twisted like giant snakes. This was the perfect place to hide.

Cherry smothered a giggle feeling quite proud of herself.

As she crouched down, she noticed the temperature drop. Goosebumps prickled her arms, and she hugged herself to stay warm. The air around her felt heavy, like it was pressing down on her small shoulders. Cherry heard a faint whisper, so soft she thought she imagined it.

"Little girl? Do you want some candy?" The voice was high-pitched, like a child's, but none of her friends were near her. Who was offering candy?

"Who's there?" Cherry whispered back, her voice trembling. There was no answer, just the rustling of leaves and the distant sound of cicadas. The little girl's heart raced, and she could feel sweat trickling down her back despite the sudden cold.

She peeked around the tree and saw something that made her blood run cold. This was no child. Not at all. She wasn't sure what she was looking at. She blinked again and fought the urge to make water.

A figure stood at the edge of the playground, half-hidden by the shadows. It was tall and dark, with eyes that seemed to glow faintly. It didn't move, just watched the children—and Cherry—silently. She glanced around for her friends, but they didn't seem to notice the Watcher.

Cherry pressed her eyes shut, blinked, and when she opened them again, the thing was gone. She rubbed her eyes, wondering if she had imagined the whole thing. She was about to call out to her friends when she heard the whisper again, closer this time.

"Cherry...I have so much candy for you..."

As she ran as fast as she could away from the strange figure and the voice, Mickey and Tonya seemed totally entranced by some bug they found.

"Look! Do you see him?" Cherry clutched Tonya's sweaty hand as she rose to her feet to stare in the direction her friend pointed.

"See what?" But Cherry was too scared to speak. Then she heard Tonya gasp and Mickey was on his feet too. "I think I see something. Mickey? What is that?" They huddled together, trying to convince themselves it was just a trick of the light, just their imaginations. But deep down, they all knew something was wrong and the park felt different, like it was alive and watching them.

The cemetery wasn't far away, right next to the playground actually, but the graves had never bothered Cherry before. Like her Momma said, those people in the ground are asleep, but this thing...it wasn't a ghost. Was it? Was one of the dead people awake?

"We should go home. It's getting dark," Mickey announced. As the lone boy in the play group, he often acted as their protector. That and he was the tallest amongst their small group of friends.

The game was forgotten, and they decided to leave, but not before one last glance back at the playground. The shadows seemed to pulse, like they were waiting for something.

As they walked away, Cherry couldn't shake the feeling that they were being watched, that whatever was in the park wasn't done with them yet. She considered taking the shortcut through the cemetery to get home quicker but decided against it.

As they left the playground, the unease didn't leave Cherry. She tried to shake it off and focus on the walk home, but the shadows seemed to follow them. The air grew colder, and the whispers, so faint before, seemed to echo in the distance. Cherry cried as she clutched Tonya's sweaty hand and refused to let it go.

"Did you hear that?" Mickey asked, his voice trembling slightly.

They all stopped, straining to listen. There it was again, a faint whisper, almost like a child's giggle, carried by the wind.

*Who wants candy? Come to me, little ones...*

Tonya clutched her hand tighter. "Are you doing that, Cherry? Mickey?" They both shook their heads and she quickly added, "Let's hurry home."

They quickened their pace, but the park felt like it was closing in around them. The trees seemed taller, their branches reaching out like skeletal fingers. The shadows moved in the corner of their eyes, and every rustle of leaves made them jump.

As Cherry reached the edge of the park, she felt a cold hand brush against her shoulder. She spun around, but there was nothing there. Just the darkening park and the ominous feeling that they were not alone.

"Come on, Cherry, we're almost out," Tonya urged, pulling her forward. Cherry stumbled, trying to keep up, her heart pounding in her young chest.

Suddenly, a thick fog began to roll in, covering the ground and swirling around their feet. The whispers grew louder, more insistent, and the giggles turned into eerie, echoing laughter.

Mickey stopped and looked around, his eyes wide with fear. "Where's the path? I can't see it!"

The children huddled together, unsure which way to go. The fog was so thick now that they could barely see a few feet ahead. The laughter grew louder, and Cherry felt like the park was closing in on them.

"Cherry, Tonya, stay close to me," Mickey said, trying to sound brave. "We'll find our way out."

But as they took a few hesitant steps forward, Tonya suddenly found her voice. "Mickey! Cherry! Help me!"

Cherry turned to see Tonya being pulled into the fog, her hands reaching out desperately for her friend. Her terrified friend screamed, but no sound came out of her mouth. How was that possible?

Mickey and Cherry grabbed her hands, and tried to pull her back, but the force in the fog was too strong.

"Help! Help us!" Cherry screamed as she cried.

It felt like the shadows themselves were dragging her away, too.

"Don't let go!" Tonya cried; her voice full of terror. But the grip on her was too strong, and slowly, she was pulled from her friends' grasp. "Cherry! Mickey! Help me!"

Then there was no sound at all, just an odd crunching sound, like someone was snapping bones, or something.

"Tonya!" Cherry screamed, trying to reach her, but it was too late. She had vanished completely into the fog, her screams echoing around them. Her bones were breaking! Her bones were breaking! "Tonya! Where are you?"

Mickey and Cherry stood frozen, unable to comprehend what had just happened. The park was silent now, the fog lifting as quickly as it had appeared. The only evidence of what had happened was the lingering fear in their hearts.

"We have to get help," Mickey said, his voice shaking. "We have to tell someone."

They ran out of the park and into the town, shouting for help. The townspeople gathered, listening to their frantic yet unbelievable story, but when they reached the park, there was no sign of Tonya.

And no sign of the fog either, or the tall, thin figure that hid inside it.

Yes, it had been a tall, slender figure, dressed in black. Cherry would never forget what he looked like. But the shadows were still, the whispers gone, and the park seemed almost normal.

Cherry knew better. The park was hiding something here in the Maple Hill Cemetery, something dark and malevolent. And it wasn't done yet.

The whole town came alive with panic and urgency. News of Tonya's disappearance spread quickly, and soon parents, neighbors, and even the local sheriff were combing every inch of the old park.

The sun dipped below the horizon, casting the park in shadows that seemed even more menacing now.

Lanterns flickered, casting ghostly light on the twisted roots and overgrown paths. The rustling leaves and distant calls of night birds added to the eerie atmosphere.

Cherry stayed close to her parents, her heart still pounding from the terror of what had happened. She refused to stay at home, her best friend was missing.

"Tonya! Tonya, where are you?" voices called out, echoing through the park. The beams of lanterns and flashlights swept through the trees, but there was no sign of the little girl.

The sheriff, a stern man with a grizzled beard, gathered a group near the swings. "We need to organize this search," he said, his voice steady but urgent. "Form lines and cover every section of the park. No stone unturned."

Cherry's father took her hand, squeezing it tightly. "Stay close, Cherry. We'll find her."

The child nodded, tears welling up in her eyes. The park felt so different now, so much more sinister. The shadows seemed to pulse with malevolent energy, and the whispers had returned, just at the edge of hearing.

As they moved through the park, Cherry caught glimpses of those same shadows flitting between the trees. The air was thick with tension and fear.

A group of men had brought dogs to help with the search, their barking filling the night. The dogs seemed uneasy, their noses to the ground but their ears pinned back, as if they sensed something unnatural.

They reached the twisted oak tree where Cherry had hidden earlier. She stared at its gnarled roots, remembering the cold touch and the whispering voice.

"It was here," she said to her father, her voice trembling. "This is where I last saw her."

The sheriff nodded, directing a few men to search the area thoroughly. They moved quickly, lifting roots, peering into hollow trunks, but there was nothing. No trace of Tonya. Only an odd ribbon that may have belonged to her. Cherry couldn't remember if she wore her ribbon in her hair that day.

Hours passed, and the sense of dread grew. The townsfolk, once hopeful, were now whispering among themselves, their faces pale and drawn. The sheriff called everyone back to the center of the park, his expression grim.

"We'll continue the search at first light," he announced. "For now, everyone should go home. We'll keep a few men here to watch the park."

The child's heart sank.

*How could they stop searching? Tonya was out there, somewhere in the darkness, needing their help. She was with the tall man, and he'd crunched her up.*

Cherry couldn't explain how she knew that, but she did. What else would have made that sound? As they made their way out of the park, Cherry glanced back one last time. The shadows seemed to be watching, the whispers were louder now, almost taunting. She shivered, knowing that whatever had taken Tonya was still out there, lurking in the darkness, waiting.

"Cherry, come on," her mother urged gently, pulling her away from the park's edge.

That night, the town was steeped in sorrow and fear. Everyone locked their doors and windows, but sleep did not come easy for anyone, especially Mickey and Cherry.

The whispers followed Cherry into her dreams, a constant reminder that the old park held secrets that it wasn't ready to reveal. And she couldn't shake the feeling that it was far from over.

She rolled over in her narrow bed, her eyes filled with blurry tears. That's when she saw Tonya floating outside her window. She was in the fog, floating and waving at her like nothing was wrong.

Nothing at all. But Cherry's bedroom was on the second floor. There were no trees close by, no way Tonya could get up there with her.

Was she dreaming? Cherry closed her eyes and counted to ten but when she opened them again, Tonya was still there. How was this possible?

Surely, she couldn't get in here. Not in her room. The window is closed! She thought about calling for her mother and father but she couldn't find her voice. She peeked over the blanket again.

Tonya wasn't alone. The tall, slender man was with her and in his hands, his bony white skeletal hands, were candies. Some she recognized, some she didn't, but she wanted none of them.

"No! Go away!" Cherry whispered as the window slid up. "No! Mommy! Help me!" But like when Tonya was captured by the monster, her voice made no sound.

*How would Mommy hear her? How would she know Cherry was in danger?*

Cherry sat up in her bed and stared in horror as the pair invaded her room. The thing with Tonya's face, fell on the floor and landed on all fours like a dog, and her bones were all broken. Cherry could hear them snapping as she moved. She wanted to scream her life away but no sound came out of her mouth. She could barely breathe; it was like an invisible hand was wrapped around her throat.

The Tall Man spoke in a deep, creepy voice, his hands outstretched, full of blood covered candy. "Pick one, dear Cherry. Pick one!"

His large hand was in front of her but she wanted nothing to do with the candy the monster offered. Finally, her voice had sound, and she screamed for her mother. By the time she quit screaming, her mother had managed to get the bedroom door open.

Sometimes the door got stuck, Mrs. Adams blamed it on the wood swelling from the humidity, but Cherry's mother was not prepared for what she saw when she and her husband fell into the room.

The window was wide open and Cherry was gone. At least, part of her was.

When her mother pulled back the covers, she found her child's body, or at least pieces of it, along with some candy wrappers.

Cherry's mother screamed until she puked.

# Chapter One–Midas

My office at Gulf Coast Paranormal headquarters was cluttered with old books and paranormal equipment, the kind of mess that only someone in my line of work would find comforting.

*Okay. Honestly, not me. This messiness wasn't like me at all.*

Here lately, I found myself feeling overwhelmed and I had no idea why.

I had just settled in with a cup of warmed-over coffee, hoping for a quiet hour or so to go through some case notes, when the phone rang. The sharp sound cut through the silence, making me jump. I sloshed coffee on my jeans. I sighed instead of swearing. I was trying to break that habit.

Swearing wasn't like me, not at all. But it was a bad habit I'd picked up lately for some reason. I wasn't good at swearing and I could tell that my wife wasn't a fan of it either, although she said nothing to me. Couldn't miss those raised eyebrows though. Nothing like an angry red head giving you the stare down.

I picked up the receiver, half-expecting another prank call or a fan seeking tickets for an upcoming event. Sierra and her para-cons. Those were on her and I reminded her of that often.

"Gulf Coast Paranormal. Midas speaking," I answered, trying to keep my voice steady and professional.

"Mr. Midas, please help me!" The voice on the other end was trembling, filled with an urgency that immediately caught my attention. "It's my child—my baby girl—she's gone! Taken by the spirits in the Dead Children's Playground!"

My heart skipped a beat. "Calm down, ma'am. Start from the beginning. What's your name?" I dabbed at my wet jeans with an old napkin before reaching for a pen and unstained paper.

"My name is Susan. Susan Harris," she said, her voice breaking. "Brody St. James told me to call you. We live in Huntsville. My daughter, Sabra, she's been missing for three days now. I know it's those spirits. I've seen things—heard things. The park is haunted, Mr. Midas. Please, you have to help us!"

I grabbed a notepad, scribbling down details as she spoke. Huntsville. Dead Children's Playground. Missing child. "Tell me about Sabra, Susan. Have you filed a missing person's report? What do the police say?"

"Yes, I did all that but they don't have a clue! I know what's happened. It got her! The thing at the park!"

I wanted to help the woman but I wasn't sure this wasn't a prank. She was crying and I could hardly understand her. As she spoke, I booted up my computer and began searching for "Sabra Harris Missing Child Huntstville." I didn't expect that anything would come up. I mean, we had our share of nuts asking for help but clearly this was no joke. My heart sunk.

Susan kept talking. "I told Sabra to stay away from that place, but you know how kids can be—stubborn. Or at least mine is, well, stubborn, kind of like I used to be. They don't listen. Sabra...she's a good kid, but she's got a mind of her own. I'm going through a divorce and it's been hard on her. Please, help us. I can't wait for these cops to find her—they don't believe me!"

It was my nature to remain calm but seeing the news articles on the computer about the missing child broke my heart. "Tell me what you know, Susan. Don't leave anything out. No matter how improbable it sounds. I need to know everything."

"Before Sabra disappeared, shadows would move at night in the house where there shouldn't be any, and I hear disembodied laughter. Or I did. It was a man's voice. I've heard it calling Sabra's name. I burned sage in the house, said some prayers before she...before this happened, but it's always cold upstairs, even in the middle of summer. It's gotten worse over the past few months. And the feeling of being watched...it's unbearable," she said, her voice a mix of fear and desperation.

"How long have you lived in the house? Was anyone with Sabra when she disappeared?"

"Six months. Just since the divorce. I don't think anyone was with her but her best friend—Felicia. But she swears she knows nothing, but I wouldn't put it past her to hide things from me. I don't really like her, she's trouble. I told Sabra that and now, my daughter is missing. What have I done?"

I paused as she wept. My heart broke for her, but I wasn't sure what to think. I was already calculating how long it would take to get there. Four hours? Five hours?

"I don't know what else to do, Mr. Midas."

"Just Midas. I'm sorry you're going through this, Susan."

"Brody said he knows you, that he met you at a convention last year. He's a local investigator but he doesn't have a team anymore. He's retired. The police don't believe me, but I know what I felt in this house. I know what took Sabra. She was trying to warn me but I...I didn't want to believe her."

A chill ran down my spine. This sounded serious. "Yes, Brody is a good guy. Wait a second. Believe in what, Susan? What did Sabra tell you?"

"Sabra said he was outside the window. The Tall Man, they call him. She said he wears a black suit, he's tall and not human. He kept whispering her name, over and over again, begging her to open the window. He's a local legend around here. These kids, they don't know what they're messing with. I caught her playing with a Ouija board. I blame Felicia for that. I would never have bought her something like that. I told her never to play with that dang thing, but then she snuck out. Snuck out the house and now she's gone. I'm no fool. Time is not on our side."

The poor mother was beside herself with fear. I didn't blame her. "Susan, I need to talk to the team. We'll come to Huntsville. We'll help in any way we can. I promise we'll do everything we can to find Sabra. Do you know the name of the detective in charge of the investigation?"

"Detective Bobby Malone, but he's not open to any of this. Believe me, I've tried to talk to him. Thank you," she sobbed. "Thank you so much."

"Do you have his number handy?" I jotted the number down, did my best to calm her fear, but I was careful not to make promises that I could not keep. I couldn't be sure we'd find the child, but we needed to try.

After hanging up, I sat back in my chair, processing what I had just heard.

This wasn't the first time I'd dealt with claims of haunted locations, but something about Susan's fear felt different—more immediate, more real. I knew we had to move quickly.

I called the team together. Cassidy, Sierra, Jericho, and Macie filed into my office, their expressions ranging from curiosity to concern. Chris hadn't responded to my text or phone call, so I didn't push the issue. Let him take off all the time he needed.

"We've got a new case," I said, laying out the details. "A pre-teen girl named Sabra has gone missing in Huntsville. Her mother is convinced it's the work of an entity at the Dead Children's Playground. She says that either the daughter snuck out of the house or she was taken."

Cassidy's eyes widened as she snapped her fingers. "Taken? By a ghost? Wait? Dead Children's Playground? I've heard of that place. It's supposed to be one of the most haunted spots in Alabama. It's next to Maple Hill Cemetery."

Jericho nodded. "Yeah, I've read about that place too. Strange disappearances dating back over a century. Little children go missing there. Or used to. This could be big. Kind of like the Slender Man, but way before that trend started. The Tall Man, that's what they call him."

A moment of silence settled over the meeting room, which we affectionately referred to as "the war room." Cassidy, Sierra, Jericho,

Joshua and Macie stared at me as I relayed the story, each carrying their own mix of curiosity and concern.

The weight of the task ahead was palpable, but I knew we had faced dark forces before. Still, this case felt different.

"Alright, here's what we know," I began, standing at the head of the table. "This case is going to require all of our skills and focus. A pre-teen girl named Sabra Harris has gone missing in Huntsville. Her mother is convinced it's the work of a malevolent spirit at Dead Children's Playground. We can't be sure that the paranormal is at fault, but the mother seems convinced that Sabra's disappearance is a result of the Tall Man that you mentioned, Jericho."

Cassidy's eyes widened in recognition. "That's right!" She snapped her fingers. "The Tall Man sightings have been common over the years. I can't believe this is happening again."

"If that's what this is. We don't know what we're up against yet." Sierra reminded us with a cryptic smile.

Jericho nodded; his expression serious. I continued, feeling the gravity of the situation settle over the room. "Susan Harris, Sabra's mother, reported seeing shadows and hearing disembodied laughter in her house. She lives close to the Maple Hill Cemetery. This thing has been haunting their home for months. There's a possibility that Sabra was seen with her friend Felicia but she's not confessing, and Susan is desperate for our help."

Macie, always the skeptic, furrowed her brow. "A lot of haunted places have legends about tall, dark figures. But if there's any chance this is real, we need to be extremely cautious. I get the feeling that the mother isn't telling us everything."

Sierra, our resident psychic, spoke up next. "She's right. I can see Sabra. She's playing with boards and pendulums. Or she was. I don't get that she's dead, but she's still in danger. We'll need all our equipment: EMF detectors, FLIR cameras, EVP recorders, and protective charms.

What about RYDER?" Sierra stared off into space as she often did when she was tuning into the invisible.

I nodded in agreement. "Good thinking, Sierra. We'll need every tool at our disposal. This might be one of the toughest cases we've faced yet. Joshua? Can you and Jericho work with RYDER on this case?"

Joshua nodded as he headed to the storeroom to get things ready.

I took a deep breath, feeling the weight of responsibility. "We'll head out ASAP. Pack your gear and be ready to leave in an hour. It's a long drive, and we need to get there as soon as possible."

Sierra immediately got on the phone to book hotel rooms. Macie and Cassidy were whispering together, sharing their suspicions.

As the team dispersed to gather their equipment, I couldn't shake the feeling that something dark and dangerous was waiting for us in Huntsville.

The image of the Tall Man, as described by Susan, lingered in my mind. But no matter what we faced, we had to uncover the truth and bring Sabra back. If it were possible.

Sierra and Cassidy's intuition led me to believe that Sabra was still alive but certainly in danger. Sierra described Sabra's feelings, "She's terrified. She's hiding in a place that she thinks is safe but the truth is..." Sierra wiped a tear away from her eye. "Nowhere is safe for her. He's coming for her because she summoned him. To make matters worse, I get the sense that this child has psychic abilities, but it could be just her age. There's another girl too. The Tall Man is going to make a play for her. She's involved somehow. How many children are missing?"

"Just Sabra at the moment, but her mother Susan did say that Sabra and her best friend Felicia were playing with a Ouija Board. She busted them and threw the board out, but we all know that's not always enough. No doubt they didn't close the session. Who knows what they did." I didn't really know what to think yet.

Sierra sighed sadly and shook her head. "These kids. They have no idea what they're playing with until it is too late."

I returned to my office, but not before making sure we packed extra batteries and double-checked our supplies. No matter how many batteries we packed lately, it never seemed to be enough. It was almost as if the paranormal activity had ramped up. Maybe it just seemed that way.

The unsettling feeling in my gut wouldn't go away, but I pushed it aside. We had a job to do, and a young girl's life was at stake. Whatever horrors awaited us, we would face them together.

It took us a bit—not the hour I commanded but all of us had families, except for Jericho and Macie. But eventually we got sitters lined up, packed our bags and met back at the office in record time. We took the largest SUV, that would be mine, as it would be roomy enough for equipment and a few suitcases.

After she put on her seatbelt, Sierra fired up her laptop and began digging into the history of the cemetery and the playground.

Beside me, Cassidy opened her sketchpad, and Jericho and Macie did some pre-game warm ups by running a spirit box session, but the results were garbled and unclear.

"Let's turn that off for now. We need to know everything we can about this place before we get there," I said, as we drove onto the highway. "Let's start with historical records and any local legends."

Sierra typed furiously on her laptop, pulling up old newspaper articles and archived records. "This park has a dark history. It's next to Maple Hill Cemetery, which is one of the oldest cemeteries in Alabama. There have been reports of children going missing dating back to the early 1900s."

Cassidy, her eyes scanning a particularly old map, nodded. "I've read about this too. The original playground was built in the 1890s, but it was abandoned and rebuilt several times. There are numerous accounts of ghostly sightings and unexplained phenomena. Some people claim to have seen a tall, dark figure lurking around the park at night. He's known as the Tall Man."

Jericho flipped through an old book, his brow furrowed. "Here's something interesting. It's a book I found at a thrift store a while back, it's called the Wicked South. In 1902, a trio of children disappeared while playing in the park. One at a time. Days apart. The community was devastated, and the bodies of the children were never found. Since then, the park has been considered cursed. Strangely enough, there are no weird stories about the cemetery, not beyond the usual."

Sierra scribbled down notes, I felt a chill run down my spine.

Joshua had been strangely quiet. "We need to understand the entity we're dealing with. The Tall Man, as he's known, might be connected to these disappearances or he might not be. We need to find out if there's a pattern or a way to communicate with the spirits trapped there."

Sierra continued her search, her fingers flying over the keyboard. "There are reports of cold spots, disembodied voices, and shadow figures. People have also experienced sudden drops in temperature and the feeling of being watched. It's classic haunting activity but on a much larger and more sinister scale."

Cassidy began sketching a rough layout of the playground, her hand moving quickly over the paper. "This is what the playground looks like based on old photographs and descriptions. We need to be strategic about where we place our equipment. We should cover the swings, the slide, and the old oak trees—those seem to be hotspots for activity."

Macie, who had been quiet until now, looked up from Jericho's book. "There's also a local legend about a man who lived near the park. Some say he lured children with candy and then...well, they were never seen again. It could be related to our Tall Man. I mean, he could be the Tall Man, just an evil dead man who is distorting his appearance to terrorize his victims. We've seen it before, right?"

I nodded, feeling the pieces of the puzzle slowly come together. "Alright, here's the plan. As I meet with Mrs. Harris, you all set up equipment around the key areas, and start our investigation as soon as we get there. We need to be thorough and cautious. This entity is dangerous, and we can't underestimate it. I called the detective in charge of this case, but he's not interested in talking to me so let's just stay out of their way."

The team nodded in agreement, a sense of determination settling over us. I couldn't shake the feeling that this case was different. More personal, more urgent. "We've got a long drive ahead of us, and time is of the essence."

As we sped down the highway, the sky darkened with storm clouds, and an ominous sense of foreboding settled over me. But I pushed it aside.

We had a job to do, and we wouldn't stop until we found Sabra and uncovered the truth behind the horrors of Dead Children's Playground.

Now that I knew the other child was in danger too, well, that made me even more sick.

I floored it.

# Chapter Two–Sierra

The drive to Huntsville was tense and quiet after our initial burst of information. But then, each of us were lost in our thoughts about what lay ahead. As we neared our destination, the dark clouds seemed to gather more thickly, casting an eerie shadow over the town.

I couldn't shake the feeling that something was watching us, waiting for us to arrive. I closed my eyes.

*Okay, Sierra. Focus.*

When we finally pulled up to Susan Harris's house, I felt a chill that had nothing to do with the weather. The house was an old Victorian, its paint peeling and windows staring blankly like empty eyes.

Susan waited for us at the door, her face pale and drawn with worry. Midas put the car in park. He and Cassidy left us to head over to the cemetery while they did the initial interview.

Normally, I was the one that did these initial interviews but not always. Sometimes it was me and Big Brother. Other times, it was Midas by himself. I was okay with Cassidy joining him.

I could *feel* that Sabra was nearby. Had she even left the house? I glanced up at it while Joshua and I moved to the front seat.

"Wait, Joshua. Let's wait for Midas and Cassidy to come back out. I want to go in that house," I whispered to him. He nodded to show that he understood. He turned off the vehicle and we both ignored Midas who glanced at us questioningly. I smiled at him, and he decided not to argue with us.

"Thank you for coming. All of you," she said, her voice barely above a whisper. "Please, come in. Wow, the whole team. Y'all come on in." She waved at us, and we happily complied. Thank you." She wiped tears away from her eyes and my heart immediately broke for her.

The inside of the house was just as unsettling. Macie and Jericho followed us inside. Shadows seemed to linger in the corners, and the air was thick with the scent of burned sage.

*Okay, so she was a believer in metaphysical world. Huh. No wonder her daughter was playing with the paranormal.*

Susan led us to the living room, where we gathered around the coffee table covered with photographs and newspaper clippings. Her phone rang and she ran to pick it up. I watched her shoulders sag.

*Okay, so not good news.*

"Newspapers, television stations. Not helpful at all so far. This is Sabra," Susan said, holding up a picture of a smiling girl with bright eyes and curly hair. "She's only twelve. She...she disappeared three days ago."

I reached out and took the photo, feeling a pang of sadness. "Sabra is gifted, isn't she?" I asked her mother.

"I guess so. I never thought about it. She's just Sabra. We're very much alike. I taught her not to be afraid of what she cannot see because I know how it feels to be misunderstood. I come from a very religious background, and I didn't want that for her. I know how it feels to see things others cannot and have nobody believe you. Sabra was seeing the Tall Man. She was drawing pictures of him before she vanished. See?" She dug in her stack of paper and reached for a few pictures.

"Hey, she's got talent," Cassidy said sweetly. "Sabra is very good. Look at this, Midas. She's quite the artist." Midas leaned over his pretty wife and studied the sketch. "Is this the Tall Man?" Susan nodded her head silently.

"Wow. She is good." Midas's voice sounded sad and a bit empty. What was going on with him? I struggled with what I wanted to tell her, that Sabra was still alive. That she was hiding because she felt afraid and guilty.

I decided not to tell her anything just yet because there was a chance I could be wrong, I didn't think I was but just in case, I kept my fat mouth shut.

"Can I take a look at her room?" I asked Susan who readily took me to the room.

It was like most any other young teen's room. There were questionable band posters on the wall. A corkboard was full of photographs, awards, various poems and things that meant something to Sabra. I touched one of the pictures and immediately saw flashes.

*Sabra running, white tennis shoes practically glowing in the dark. She was up, high. Like in a tree house. She was hiding and she believed she was in trouble. Terror. I feel terror. No, she was feeling this. She is alive! I can feel it!*

"Sabra," I whispered her name as her mother hovered in the doorway. I couldn't hide this from her. I had to ask questions. "Did Sabra ever have a tree house? Or is there a tree she likes to climb? Maybe in your backyard or at the playground?"

Susan's eyes widened at my questions. "We used to have a tree house, at our old house, where she grew up. We moved here after my divorce. Jim, that's my ex-husband, he's on deployment. He's overseas but the house is empty. Oh God! You think she's at Jim's place? I have the keys. I'm sure Jim wouldn't care if we went to check it out. I can't get a hold of him, he's...well, overseas. He's in the military but we're not really speaking. Divorce. Need I say more."

Midas interceded here. "Do the police know about the other house? About your ex being deployed? That Sabra might be there? Sierra, are you picking up Sabra?"

"Does that mean she's dead?" Susan's hand flew to her mouth.

I raised my hand to calm her. "No. She's alive but she's hiding. She's afraid of this thing, afraid of getting into trouble," Macie touched Susan's arm briefly but quickly removed it. Her face revealed something, I knew that as Macie's warm brown eyes met mine. Yeah, she had picked up on something.

"Oh God! You think so? Um, yes. I mean, I did tell the police about Jim and I. I also told them about the other house. Maybe not the tree house though. Do you think she's there? Oh my God! That makes perfect sense! I knew it! She's alive! My Sabra is alive! I would have felt it if she was gone. Wouldn't I? A mother would know!"

Midas decided that he would go with her to Jim's house, and I volunteered to stay with the rest of the team. Midas insisted that we call the police first before trespassing on Jim's private property.

The detective agreed to meet them there and we were eager to get started on our investigation. Even if Sabra was found, I could sense the evil in the Harris house.

*Yeah, the Tall Man was real and quite evil. He had been here before. Yes, he knew this house. He knew it very well.*

Before he left he pulled me to the side. "Are you sure about what you saw, Little Sister? I hate to break this woman's heart."

"Midas. Really? If you don't trust me by now," I couldn't believe he would question my abilities. "I wouldn't have said it if I didn't believe it. Sabra is alive but she's not out of the woods yet. This entity, he wants her." Joshua stood beside me, his hand on my shoulder. I was both glad and irritated for his presence.

"I wasn't insinuating you were intentionally misleading the client, Sierra Kay. I'm sorry I said anything. You guys head to the park. I'll keep you posted on what we find," Midas said before walking off. What was his problem?

Joshua continued to stand beside me as we watched Midas leave with Susan.

We'd locked the house up and loaded back into the SUV. Nobody said much. Midas rode away in Susan's vehicle; I was surprised to see that Cassidy didn't go with him.

I couldn't shake the feeling that Big Brother was going through something. Something I didn't understand.

*Mind your own business, Sierra Kay.*

The park was not far but it was eerie in the fading light, the swings creaking in the breeze and the slide glistened, proof that the equipment was new. We set up our gear quickly, placing EMF detectors and EVP recorders around the playground.

It was hard to ignore that the Dead Children's Playground was butted up against the Maple Hill Cemetery. It was a lovely cemetery, kind of hilly with lots of neat statuary but not everyone was at rest.

I pretended that I didn't see the restless dead. It wouldn't last long; it was always difficult to fake it for very long. I prayed they stayed away.

I focused on setting up the FLIR camera near an old oak tree that Cassidy had identified as a hotspot. As I adjusted the settings, I felt a sudden drop in temperature. My breath puffed out in front of me in small, white clouds.

"Guys, I've got a temperature drop over here," I called out. "Geesh. I'm freezing."

Macie and Jericho joined me, their expressions serious. "Let's run an EVP session here," Macie suggested.

We gathered around the tree, and Macie started asking questions. "Is anyone here with us? Can you tell us your name?"

For a moment, there was nothing but the sound of the wind rustling the leaves. Then, a faint whisper came through the recorder. "Help us...Mickey."

The hair on the back of my neck stood up. "Did you hear that?" I whispered.

Jericho nodded, his face pale. "Yeah, I heard it. Let's play it back. I heard a name."

We listened to the recording again, and the whisper was clear as day. "Help us...Mickey."

My heart raced. "There's definitely something here," I said, feeling both fear and determination. "We need to keep going."

As we moved around the playground, the temperature continued to drop, and the EMF detectors started to spike. We captured more EVPs, most of them faint whispers asking for help or calling out names.

It was clear that the spirits of children were still here, trapped and desperate. But again, I didn't pick up on Sabra Harris. I didn't pick up on anyone recently dead, except for some of those spirits wandering the cemetery.

We were reviewing our findings near the swings when I saw it—a shadowy figure at the edge of the playground, watching us silently.

My blood ran cold. "Joshua, look," I whispered, pointing.

He turned, his eyes widening as he saw the figure. "The Tall Man," he breathed. He immediately pointed his IR camera in that direction but the figure didn't move, just stood there, its eyes glowing faintly in the darkness.

I felt an overwhelming sense of dread, like we were in the presence of something truly evil.

"Should we approach it?" Joshua asked, his voice shaky.

Jericho shook his head. "No, not yet. We need more information. He's checking us out. I get the feeling that he's looking for Sabra. I think you're right, Sierra. She's a sensitive but why would he be so focused on her?"

The figure vanished as suddenly as it had appeared, leaving us in an unsettling silence. I had an inkling as to what the answer might be, but I didn't mention it. Assuming things was always a bad idea.

I didn't tell them about the Ouija board under Sabra's bed or her secret journal tucked under her mattress. She was a child with gifts, but she was also a child with no direction. I didn't blame her mother; I didn't blame her at all.

Evil is attracted to innocence. Sabra was a curious child, and she didn't have a clue as to how to get out of this trouble.

*Please, God. Let them find her alive. I do feel her essence.*

Despite the encounter, we knew we couldn't back down. Dead children were crying out for help. This Tall Man, he was back and we had to figure out why.

Cassidy's cell phone rang, and we all jumped. It was so quiet in the park, until the phone began to jangle. "Hey! You did? They found her! She was right where you said, Sierra. In the tree house!"

I breathed a sigh of relief. I mean, I knew they would but still, it was always felt good to bring good news to a client.

"Oh, thank God. They found her! Joshua! They found her!" I hugged him and practically wept. "Midas is going to meet us at back at Susan's house. Let's pack it up, call it a night. We need to debrief and review what we've got already."

With unexpected joy, we packed up our equipment, ready to return the next day for a more in-depth investigation.

As we left the playground, the whispers of the children's voices lingered in the air, a haunting reminder of the mystery we had to solve. I wasn't sure if anyone else could hear them, so I didn't ask. But I felt a mix of fear and determination.

We drove back to Susan's house in silence, each of us lost in our thoughts. As we pulled up, I looked at the dark house and a quickly spotted a shadowy figure standing in an upstairs window. Midas was waiting for us, along with three cop cars.

I immediately felt sick. This child wasn't out of the woods yet.

I practically jumped out of the vehicle. "They can't stay here. He's coming again for Sabra. He's not going to give up," I blurted out my thoughts without thinking.

"I figured as much," Midas added. He eased me to the side away from the investigators who were talking to Sabra and Susan. "I'll tell her. She's already called her ex-husband. Jim says they can stay at the old house. I think you're right; that's best for now and she's willing to let us investigate for a few days. Maybe we can help banish this thing. He's been here along time."

I nodded in agreement as I adjusted my sloppy bun. "Tomorrow, I want to talk to her, Sabra I mean. I have questions. The child is gifted. She needs to know how to protect herself."

That night, as I lay in bed at the hotel, I couldn't sleep.

The image of the Tall Man haunted my thoughts, and the whispers of the children's voices echoed in my mind.

*Oh, so many children. He's taken so many, so many that were never found.*

"Sierra, you've barely closed your eyes. What's going on? Talk to me? Is it Midas?"

"No. It's not about Midas. It's this thing, the Tall Man, this entity, he hides in the fog. He hides in the shadows. He feels connected to Sabra. He wants her because he's spiritually weak. He's starving. He wants to feed on her." I hated saying such things, but it was the truth.

I knew we were up against something truly evil, but I also knew we wouldn't stop until we found the other missing children and freed *all* the spirits trapped in Dead Children's Playground.

Sabra was safe and sound but the others were still missing.

I could hear them crying in the night, crying for help.

It was a cry that I would answer.

# Chapter Three–Cassidy

The next morning, the team and I gathered in the dimly lit hotel restaurant, the soft murmur of early risers and the clinking of silverware blending into a strangely comforting background noise.

Midas hadn't spoken much, not even to me. I wanted to know what was on his mind, but I knew my husband well enough to know he'd tell me when he was ready.

The air was thick with the smell of bacon, eggs, and freshly brewed coffee, but there was an unsettling tension that none of us could shake. We had spent the night at a relatively cheap hotel because there wasn't much else available. Apparently, there was some convention in town, so all the nicer spots were full. *But hey, any port in a storm, right?*

This morning each of us seemed lost in our own thoughts about the investigation ahead. Was it over? I mean, there was still the mystery of the Tall Man.

As I sipped my stale coffee, I glanced around at the others. Midas was nursing his own cup, his brow furrowed in thought. Sierra and Joshua were deep in conversation, their voices low, while Macie absentmindedly pushed her food around on her plate. Jericho was texting on his phone.

None of us had slept well. How could we, with the horrors of Dead Children's Playground still fresh in our minds?

A flicker of movement drew my attention to the television mounted on the wall. The news anchor's voice was muted, but the headline scrolling across the bottom of the screen caught my eye: MISSING GIRL SABRA HARRIS FOUND ALIVE.

I nearly dropped my coffee cup, my heart skipping a beat. "Look!" I said, pointing to the TV. Everyone turned to see the headline.

Midas grabbed the remote from the nearby table and turned up the volume, his face a mix of surprise and relief. The reporter's voice filled the room, clear and tinged with emotion. "In breaking news,

Sabra Harris, the twelve-year-old girl who went missing three days ago, was found alive late last night near Maple Hill Cemetery. Sources say she was disoriented but unharmed. Authorities are investigating the circumstances of her disappearance, but so far, no foul play has been confirmed."

Relief flooded through me, but it was quickly tempered by confusion. "Poor kid," I sighed, my voice hushed with disbelief. "I'm so grateful you picked up on her, Sierra. You did a great job."

Jericho shook his head slowly, his eyes fixed on the screen. "My grandmother is praying for us. Says to tell you that Sherman won't eat. Are you sure you sent the right food?"

Macie frowned at that question. "Sherman is a notoriously picky eater. I only ever buy him Tender Bites. If he's not eating, it's not because of the food. My poor dog. He has separation anxiety. Tell Granny he will eat when he's truly hungry. I hope he's behaving."

Jericho sent another text to his grandmother. "She says she'll try again. Her old Tom cat might be stressing him out."

"He's such a big baby," Macie chuckled before she kissed his cheek. "I'll have to do something nice for your grandmother."

Midas set the remote down, his expression serious. "Thank God Sabra's alive, which is a miracle, but we still don't know what happened to her. And that means we're not done here."

Macie leaned forward, her voice low and tense. "Sabra drew the Tall Man." The thought sent a chill down my spine. The Tall Man—just the name made my skin crawl. "Maybe she can tell us what happened."

Midas nodded. "Exactly. We need to talk to her as soon as possible. But we also need to be careful. If the Tall Man is real, he might not be done with her—or with us."

I swallowed hard, feeling the weight of his words. "So, what's the plan?"

Midas looked around the table, his gaze steady. "We split up. I'll go to the hospital to speak with Sabra, see if she can remember anything useful. Her mother took her their last night. The kid is a wreck and of course, nobody believes her, except her mother. The rest of you head back to Dead Children's Playground and start setting up for a deeper investigation. We need to figure out what we're dealing with before anyone else gets hurt."

A heavy silence settled over the table as we all absorbed his words. The relief that Sabra was alive was palpable, but it was tinged with the ominous realization that something dark and dangerous was still out there.

The Tall Man was lurking in the shadows, and we were the only ones who could stop him.

As we finished our breakfast, the image of Sabra being found alive played over and over on the TV screen, a beacon of hope in an otherwise grim situation. But I couldn't shake the feeling that this was far from over. We had a job to do, and this time, we couldn't afford any mistakes.

The morning light streamed through the restaurant windows, but it did little to chase away the darkness that clung to us. We were walking into the unknown, and we knew we had to be ready for whatever came next.

After Midas laid out the plan, the tension around the table seemed to ease slightly, though the sense of urgency was still palpable.

We knew we had to move quickly, but the thought of heading back to that playground, with the Tall Man still lurking somewhere in the shadows, was unsettling. I was torn. I really wanted to hang out with Midas, but Sierra spoke up first.

Sierra leaned forward, her eyes serious. "Midas, I think I should go with you to talk to Sabra. If she's disoriented, it might help to have a woman there, someone she can relate to. Plus, I might be able to pick up on something—anything—that could give us more clues about what she experienced."

Midas considered her words, his brow furrowing in thought. "You might be right, Sierra. Sabra's been through something traumatic, and she might respond better with you there. It could help to have another set of eyes and ears."

I watched the exchange, my coffee cooling in my hands.

Sierra was always good at reading people, picking up on details that the rest of us might miss. It made sense for her to go, but it also meant splitting up the team, which never sat well with me. Still, there wasn't time to debate it.

Not only that, but Midas also wasn't even acting like he wanted me to go. What was going on with us? Why did I feel so teary eyed? I fought the tears by going to refresh my sorry coffee.

Macie nodded, pushing her plate aside. "While you two go to the hospital, the rest of us will head back to Dead Children's Playground. We can discretely set up the equipment and also look at the older parts of the cemetery that butts up against the playground."

Jericho glanced at his phone, still texting his grandmother about Sherman. "I'm good with that. The sooner we get set up, the sooner we can figure out what's really going on here. Of course, it's an actual playground so we can expect to see families. We don't want to scare anyone."

Midas looked at me, a silent question in his eyes. "You okay, Cassidy?"

I forced a smile, though the unease was still gnawing at me. "Yeah, I'm good. We'll be careful."

He nodded, satisfied with the plan. His dark eyes met mine for a moment. *I loved this man so much. I prayed that whatever he was going through, he'd confide in me soon.* I welcomed his kiss, even though it was brief.

"Alright, then. Let's get moving. Sierra and I will head to the hospital right away. The rest of you, be safe out there. And keep your eyes open—if the Tall Man is real, we need to be ready for anything."

We all stood; the remnants of breakfast left forgotten on the table. As we gathered our gear, I felt a heavy weight settle on my shoulders. Sabra had been found, but that didn't mean the danger was over. If anything, it felt like we were only just beginning to uncover the true horror of what we were dealing with.

Midas and Sierra exchanged a quick glance before heading out the door, their faces set with determination. I watched them go, a knot of anxiety tightening in my chest.

I had a bad feeling about this, but I kept it to myself. We all had a role to play, and there was no turning back now.

*I love you, Midas Demopolis.*

As Jericho, Macie, Joshua and I made our way to the SUV, the morning sun did little to warm the cold dread that had settled deep inside me. Midas and Sierra had called for an Uber. I knew we should have taken two vehicles.

The playground and cemetery awaited us, and with them, the secrets of the Tall Man.

But we were Gulf Coast Paranormal, and this was what we did—no matter how terrifying the shadows we faced might be.

We arrived at Dead Children's Playground under a sky that was too bright for the heaviness in my chest.

The playground was eerily quiet, the swings hanging limp and lifeless, and the rusted slide reflecting the weak morning sunlight. It felt like a place forgotten by time, where laughter had once echoed but now only whispers remained. As nice as it looked, there was no one there. But it was still early in the day.

Jericho, Macie, Joshua, and I moved quickly, unloading the equipment from the van.

We had done this hundreds of times before, but today, everything felt heavier—like the very air was pressing down on us.

"Let's set up near the swings," Jericho suggested, his voice low as he glanced around the playground. "If the reports are true, that's where a lot of the activity has been concentrated."

I nodded, feeling the tension around us. Jericho's normally steady hands were shaking slightly as he unpacked the EMF detectors and EVP recorders.

Macie and Joshua moved to the edge of the playground, where the cemetery loomed just beyond a line of ancient oaks. The graves there were old, many of them covered in moss and ivy, their inscriptions worn away by time.

As I set up my sketchpad, I couldn't shake the feeling that we were being watched. The shadows seemed to shift and sway, though the breeze was barely enough to stir the leaves. A brief moment of dizziness struck me, but I closed my eyes and took a deep breath. I quickly recovered.

I glanced over at Jericho, who was adjusting one of the recorders.

"Do you think we'll get anything today?" I asked, my voice barely above a whisper. "I don't feel right. I feel off."

He looked at me, his expression serious. "I get that too. But honestly, I don't know what to expect. This place...it's different. It's a weird place, energy wise. I sense there's a lot of activity here. Not the typical energy for a resting place. It's a beautiful cemetery but I wouldn't want to be buried here. Not this close this playground, at any rate."

We finished setting up the equipment, and Jericho took a deep breath. "I'm going to read off the names of the missing children," he said, holding a small notebook in his hand. "Maybe it'll trigger something, get them to reach out to us."

I watched as he moved to the center of the playground, his voice steady as he began reading the names aloud. "Amelia Brown. David Thompson. Sarah Whitfield..."

The names hung in the air, each one a reminder of the lives lost to this place.

As Jericho continued, I felt a chill run down my spine. The temperature seemed to drop, and the hairs on the back of my neck stood on end. A car pulled up, a woman sat alone in the car watching us.

*Ugh. I got a bad feeling about her.*

Macie and Joshua were by the cemetery now, setting up the thermal cameras. I could see the tension in their movements, the way they kept glancing over their shoulders, as if expecting something to emerge from the shadows.

As Jericho finished reading the last name, Candy Adams, the silence that followed was almost suffocating. We all stood there, waiting, listening—hoping for a sign.

Then, just as I was about to speak, a soft, almost inaudible whisper drifted through the air.

"Help us..."

I froze, my heart pounding in my chest. "Did you hear that?" I whispered. "A child's voice!" I clutched the pencil a bit too tightly and accidentally snapped it.

Jericho nodded, his face pale. "Yeah, I heard it. We're not alone here."

I swallowed hard and focused on my sketchpad, letting the pencil glide across the paper. I didn't know what I was drawing, only that the lines and shapes seemed to form themselves, almost as if guided by an unseen hand.

Tonya Jakes? Is this you? No...this little girl, she wasn't Tonya. She had a different name.

The face that emerged on the page was haunting—pale, with wide, sorrowful eyes and a mouth twisted in fear. It was the face of a child, but not one I recognized. My hands trembled as I continued to sketch, unable to stop.

"Who are you?" I whispered, more to myself than to anyone else. I heard nothing else.

The air around us seemed to thicken, the shadows growing darker, deeper. How is this possible? It's mid-morning. I could feel the spirits pressing in, as if the playground itself was trying to consume us. Jericho took a step closer to me, his hand hovering protectively over the EMF detector.

"We need to stay sharp," he said quietly, his eyes scanning the area. "Whatever's here, it's close."

I nodded, my gaze flicking between the sketchpad and the playground.

The feeling of being watched was stronger now, almost unbearable. I could sense the presence of the children, their fear, their desperation. But there was something else too—something darker, more malevolent.

"Holy crap!" I couldn't help but blurt it out.

*The Tall Man!*

He was here, hovering in the shadows, watching, waiting. I could feel his eyes on us, cold and unfeeling. The fear that gripped me was unlike anything I had ever experienced before, but I knew we couldn't turn back now. He couldn't fully reveal himself as it was daytime but oh, if we returned tonight, he'd put on a show.

*Yes, I'll put on a wonderful show...do you like candy? I have some special candy for sweet girls like you.*

"Keep going," I whispered to Jericho, my voice trembling. "He's talking to me. Can you hear his voice?"

Jericho nodded; his jaw set with determination. "I hear the voice but I can't make it out. We need to be careful. He's here—I can feel him."

"The woman in the car, Jericho. She's watching us," I pointed out the voyeur who suddenly decided to spin out and leave us alone in the playground. "Bad juju. She's not a friend." As we continued our investigation, the shadows seemed to close in around us, the air growing colder with each passing moment.

The Tall Man was out there, still lurking in the sporadic darkness, and I knew that a confrontation with him was inevitable.

But we were Gulf Coast Paranormal, and this was what we did. No matter how terrifying the shadows we faced might be, we had to uncover the truth and bring peace to the lost souls trapped in this place.

Even if it meant facing the darkness head on.

I began scratching on the pad again.

He wanted me to draw him. The Tall Man.

Tears streamed down my face as my hands worked. This wasn't what I wanted to draw. Not at all, but I had no choice.

When I finally finished I threw down the sketchpad.

I hoped I never had to pick it up again.

# Chapter Four–Macie

The morning sun had climbed higher in the sky, but it did little to warm the eerie chill that clung to Dead Children's Playground. The equipment, stood like sentinels of forgotten memories, their shadows stretching long and twisted across the uneven ground.

I shivered, though it wasn't cold, not really. It was the kind of chill that seeped into your bones, the kind that came from something unnatural, something wrong. I glanced up at the clouds that had gathered dark and tall.

As we continued our investigation, I wandered away from the group, my instincts pulling me toward a patch of dirt near the swings.

The ground here looked disturbed, as if something—or someone—had been digging. I crouched down, brushing away the loose earth with my gloved hands, and that's when I saw it.

An old, weathered doll lay partially buried in the dirt, its porcelain face cracked and dirty, one eye missing.

Its once-white dress was now yellowed and tattered, the fabric fragile and brittle from years of neglect. I gently lifted it from the ground, my heart pounding in my chest.

"Hey, Jericho, come look at this," I called out, my voice hushed. "Joshua! Cassidy!"

Jericho was by my side in an instant, his eyes narrowing as he studied the doll in my hands. "That's not something you see every day," he murmured, his tone laced with unease. "That looks pretty old."

I nodded, feeling a deep sense of dread settle over me. "It feels...wrong," I said quietly. "Like it shouldn't be here. Like it's...waiting. Oh my gosh! I know better than to pick something up. Remember the Leaf Academy?"

Jericho frowned, glancing around the playground. "It's not like that, Macie. I swear. This toy was left behind for a reason. This isn't a gift.

Let's do an EVP session here, see if we can pick up anything. This might be a trigger object."

We quickly set up the EVP recorder, the device's tiny red light blinking steadily as it began to capture the sounds around us. Jericho asked the usual questions, his voice calm and steady, though I could see the tension in his shoulders.

"Is anyone here with us?" he asked. "Can you tell us your name? Is this your doll?"

For a moment, there was nothing but the sound of the wind rustling through the trees and the distant calls of birds. But then, faintly, almost imperceptibly, I heard it—a soft whine, followed by the moving of the leaves in the trees. The whine was faint, as if coming from far away, but it sent a chill down my spine.

"Did you hear that?" I whispered, my heart racing.

Jericho nodded, his eyes wide with surprise. "Yeah, I heard something. Let's play it back." He rewound the recorder, and the four of us listened in tense silence. The laughter was there, clear and unmistakable, followed by something else—something that made my blood run cold.

"Tonya," a voice whispered, so soft it was almost lost in the static. Joshua grinned and encouraged him to rewind it. Sure enough, we caught the voice.

My breath caught in my throat. "Jericho, did you hear that? It said 'Tonya."

Jericho's face paled, and he quickly pulled out the list of names he had been reading earlier. "Tonya...here she is," he said, his voice barely above a whisper. "Tonya Jakes. She disappeared in 1902. Her body was never found. The following day, one of her friends was found murdered. Her name was Cherry Adams. This thing seems to attack in clusters."

I stared at the doll in my hands, the sense of dread growing stronger. "Could this have been her doll? Maybe...maybe she's trying to tell us something."

Jericho nodded; his expression grim. "It's possible that it's Tonya. But if she's reaching out to us, it means she's still here trapped. We need to find out what happened to her, and why she's still lingering in this place."

I felt a shiver run down my spine as I carefully set the doll down on the ground, its cracked face staring up at me with an eerie, lifeless gaze.

Her name echoed in my mind; a haunting reminder of the lost souls trapped in this cursed playground. As we prepared to continue the investigation, I couldn't shake the feeling that Tonya was watching us, waiting for us to uncover the truth of her fate.

*Poor child. We're here to help you, Tonya.*

I knew, deep down, that we were getting closer to something—something dark and terrible, something that had claimed the lives of countless children.

But we had to keep going. We had to find out what happened to Tonya, and why the Tall Man still haunted this area, feeding on the fear of the innocent.

No matter how terrifying the shadows became, we couldn't turn back now. We had just finished packing up the EVP recorder when the first distant rumble of thunder rolled across the sky.

I glanced up, noticing how the clouds had thickened and darkened, their ominous presence casting an even gloomier shadow over the playground.

"Guys, I think we're about to get hit with a storm," Jericho said, his voice tense as he scanned the horizon. The once-quiet morning had turned ominous, and I felt a prickling unease crawling up my spine.

"We need to grab the gear and get out of here," I said, already moving toward the equipment. The air was thick, charged with electricity, and I could feel the first hints of static raising the hairs on my arms.

*Geesh, this was definitely a supernatural storm. Trippy.*

The wind picked up suddenly, whipping through the trees with a wild, frantic energy that sent leaves swirling around us.

Joshua, always practical, moved quickly, his focus entirely on securing the most expensive and delicate equipment. "I've got the thermal camera!" he shouted over the rising wind, his voice barely audible. "Macie! Grab the light strip!" I raced to pick it up off the ground.

The sky cracked open with a jagged streak of lightning, followed immediately by a deafening clap of thunder that shook the ground beneath our feet. The storm had arrived with a vengeance, and it was clear we had no time to waste.

"Move, now!" Jericho barked, his voice cutting through the howling wind like a whip.

The playground seemed to come alive in the chaos, the swings creaking and groaning as if unseen hands were pushing them, and the slide shuddering violently with each gust, as though something malevolent was trying to shake it loose.

We bolted toward the SUV, the sky above us boiling with black, roiling clouds that churned like a cauldron of malevolent intent. The air crackled with electricity, and the first drops of rain splattered against the ground—large, heavy, and cold as ice, hitting the earth with a force that felt like a warning, or perhaps a curse.

I could barely see through the sheets of rain that suddenly poured down, soaking us within seconds. The dirt beneath our feet turned to mud, making it difficult to keep our footing as we scrambled toward the vehicle.

"Come on, hurry!" I shouted, my voice almost drowned out by the roar of the storm.

Joshua was right behind me, clutching the equipment to his chest as if it were a lifeline. Cassidy was on his heels. Just as we reached the SUV, a blinding flash of lightning struck the ground nearby, too close for comfort. I think we all swore in a strange chorus.

The sound was deafening, and for a split second, the entire playground was illuminated in an eerie, white light. I fumbled with the door handle, my hands shaking as I tried to get inside.

Finally, the door gave way, and I tumbled into the backseat, my heart pounding in my chest.

Jericho and Joshua were right behind me, slamming the doors shut just as the storm unleashed its full force. The rain came down in torrents, pounding against the roof of the SUV like a thousand tiny hammers.

Joshua let out a breath he'd been holding, wiping the rain from his face. "We got everything," he panted, holding up the equipment he'd managed to save.

"Barely," Jericho muttered, his eyes wide as he stared out at the storm raging around us. "That was close."

"What the hell was that? This feels wrong. Supernatural storm, guys. I bet anything that's what that woman was doing here, trying to stop us. She was a dark magic practitioner, for sure." Cassidy sounded unsure; her long red hair was drenched.

Nobody asked him a practitioner of what. It couldn't be good. I sure didn't have an answer. All I could do was sit there, trembling, as the storm battered the SUV. Jericho clutched my hand and I squeezed it for comfort. The playground was now a blur outside the windows, distorted by the sheets of rain and the occasional flash of lightning.

But even in the chaos, I couldn't shake the feeling that something was out there, watching us. The Tall Man...or something worse. The storm had come out of nowhere, too sudden, too violent to be natural. It felt like a warning, or maybe even a threat.

"This place...it's not safe. I feel like we're sitting ducks."

Jericho nodded in agreement but none of us moved. I swallowed hard, watching as the playground faded into the distance. The storm showed no signs of letting up, and with each passing second, the dread in my chest grew stronger.

We had uncovered something dark, something that didn't want us here. I couldn't shake the feeling that we had only just begun to understand the true horror of what we were up against.

We sat in the SUV, the storm raging around us, each of us too shaken to speak. The rain pounded on the roof like an unrelenting barrage, and the wind howled as if it were alive, filled with malevolent intent.

My heart was still racing, my mind unable to shake the feeling that something was out there watching us, waiting for the right moment to strike.

Jericho, always the one to act, reached into the backseat and grabbed the FLIR camera.

"I need to see what's out there," he muttered, more to himself than to anyone else. He powered on the camera, its screen flickering to life with a dull, ghostly light. It was pretty dark out at the moment. There was a possibility that he might catch someone.

"Hit record, Jericho," Joshua reminded him. He did just that.

I watched him as he scanned the storm-drenched playground through the infrared lens, the tension in the air so thick it was almost suffocating. The camera hummed quietly, its sensors picking up heat signatures in the distance, but the storm made everything look distorted, surreal.

"What do you see?" I asked, my voice trembling with the fear I was trying to keep at bay.

Jericho's brow furrowed, his eyes narrowing as he focused on something in the distance.

"There's something moving out there," he said, his tone low and filled with unease. "It's not an animal... It's too tall, too...wrong. It looks that car is driving around the cemetery. It's really hard to see anything with this crazy rain."

He adjusted the camera's focus, and I leaned in closer, my breath fogging the window as I peered into the nightmarish world beyond.

The screen showed a shadowy figure moving among the trees, its form elongated and unnatural, almost like it was stretching to reach us.

My stomach churned with dread. "The Tall Man?" I whispered, barely able to speak the words.

Jericho didn't answer right away, his gaze locked on the figure as it moved closer, weaving between the trees with an unnerving fluidity. "Maybe," he said finally, his voice tight with tension. "Or something."

As we watched in horrified silence, a sudden, piercing sound cut through the storm—a child's voice, high-pitched and desperate, calling out from the darkness.

"Help me..."

My blood ran cold. The voice was faint, almost drowned out by the wind and rain, but it was clear enough to send a shiver down my spine. "Did you hear that?" I gasped, my hand flying to my mouth.

Joshua nodded, his eyes wide with fear. "It sounded like a kid...out there in this storm. But that's impossible, right? He's trying to lure us out. Nobody move."

Before anyone could respond, a strange sensation washed over me, something I hadn't felt in a long time—a pull, a compulsion to write.

"I must write. I'm getting something!"

My hand trembled as I reached for my notebook, the pen seeming to move on its own as I opened it to a blank page.

"What's happening?" Cassidy asked, her voice laced with concern as she watched me.

"I don't know," I whispered, my hand already moving across the page, the pen scratching out words in a language I didn't recognize. It wasn't English, and it wasn't anything I could consciously comprehend, but the words flowed through me as if channeled from somewhere else—somewhere dark and ancient.

Jericho glanced at the writing, his expression darkening. "That's not good, Macie. Whatever you're channeling...be careful."

I couldn't stop, even if I wanted to. The words spilled out in a frantic, desperate rush, filling the page with symbols and glyphs that seemed to pulse with an ominous energy. My heart pounded in my chest, and I felt a cold sweat break out on my forehead.

The child's voice echoed again, this time closer, more insistent. "Help me..."

The shadowy figure on the FLIR camera was almost at the edge of the trees now, its form blending with the darkness in a way that made my skin crawl. The storm raged on, but all I could focus on was the voice and the writing, both pulling me deeper into a place I didn't want to go.

Just when I thought I couldn't take it anymore, Cassidy's phone rang, the shrill sound cutting through the tension like a knife. I jumped, the pen slipping from my fingers as she fumbled to answer it.

"Midas?" she asked, her voice shaky. "I've got you on speaker. Go ahead."

"Hey guys," he said, his tone calm but urgent. "We're at the Harris house. Sierra and I have learned some things. You need to meet us here as soon as possible. You're not safe in that playground."

I glanced at Jericho, who was still watching the shadowy figure on the FLIR camera. "Yeah, we kind of figured that. Midas, there's something out here. It's close."

"I know," he replied, his voice grim. "That's why you need to leave—now. Whatever you've found there, it's connected to what we're dealing with here. Just get out of there and meet us. We'll figure this out together."

Cassidy nodded, even though Midas couldn't see her. "We're on our way." She hung up, her hands still shaking as she relayed the message to the others. "You heard him. Midas says we need to go to the Harris house. Now."

Jericho finally lowered the FLIR camera, his face pale but resolute. "Then let's go. Whatever's out there...we're not ready to face it alone."

We didn't need any more convincing. As Joshua started the SUV and pulled away from the playground, I couldn't help but look back, my eyes searching the darkness for any sign of the shadowy figure.

But all I saw was the storm, the rain falling in sheets, obscuring everything in a shroud of impenetrable darkness.

And somewhere in that darkness, I knew the Tall Man was watching us, waiting for his next move.

We didn't have long to wait.

# Chapter Five–Mickey



*Huntsville, 1902*

The moon hung high in the night sky, casting long, eerie shadows over the streets of Huntsville. The town was quiet, save for the occasional creak of a wooden shutter in the breeze.

Inside a modest house on the outskirts of town, seven-year-old Mickey sat on the edge of the rickety couch, his small body trembling with fear.

It had been days since that dreadful afternoon in Dead Children's Playground. Days since Tonya had vanished into the fog, and Cherry had been found dead in her bed, her small body twisted and broken.

Mickey had seen things—terrible, unexplainable things—but no one believed him. Not the investigating officers, and certainly not his father. If his mother was alive, she would have believed him. She would have believed every word, but she was gone. She'd been gone for quite a long time. So long, Mickey could barely remember what she looked like, and his father had taken down her portrait. Mickey tried to sneak a peek at the portrait occasionally, but he always got caught and always got in trouble.

"Mickey, enough of these lies," his father, Arthur, had said earlier that evening, his voice a low growl as he paced the living room. "There's no such thing as a Tall Man. You're just scared and confused, boy. A girl is dead! Where is Tonya? I demand that you tell me!"

But Mickey wasn't confused. He had seen the Tall Man with his own eyes—seen him lurking at the edge of the playground, his white, featureless face smiling that horrible, twisted smile. And now, every time he closed his eyes, Mickey saw him again, felt his cold presence creeping closer.

"Go to your room and stay there. You'll have to be punished." Mickey's father slung back the remnants of his whiskey and began tugging at his belt. Mickey knew what was coming for him. His father was a cruel man, even on the best of days. This was not a best day or even a good one.

Mickey's friends were dead. He was sure that Tonya was dead too. Mickey raced upstairs, tears in his young eyes, a prayer on his lips. He prayed that it was just a few slaps, not a drunken beating.

The door to his room creaked open, and Mickey flinched, his wide eyes snapping to the figure standing in the doorway. It was his father as promised, belt in hand, his face twisted with anger.

"I warned you, Mickey," Arthur said, his voice dangerously low. "I warned you to stop lying. But you just had to keep on, didn't you? Your mother was a liar too. She said she wouldn't leave me but she's gone. Gone and left you behind. She could have at least taken you with her."

"She's dead, Pa! I'm sorry!" Mickey's heart pounded in his chest as he scrambled back on the bed, his small hands clutching the worn blanket. "But it's true, Pa! I swear! The Tall Man was there! He took Tonya, and he hurt Cherry! I saw him! He's a monster!"

Arthur's eyes darkened, and he took a step closer, the belt dangling ominously from his hand. "Enough!" he bellowed. "You're going to learn what happens to liars in this house!"

"I'm not lying, Pa. I swear I saw him! He's a monster with long arms and legs."

Tears welled up in Mickey's eyes as he pressed himself against the headboard, his body shaking with fear. But as Arthur loomed closer, something caught Mickey's eye—something in the shadows behind his father.

*The Tall Man.*

He stood there, impossibly tall and thin, his black suit blending into the darkness, his featureless white face glowing faintly in the dim light. How had he gotten in here?

His smile, wide and malevolent, stretched impossibly across his face, and his long, bony fingers twitched at his sides as if eager to reach out and grab Mickey.

Mickey's breath caught in his throat, his eyes widening in terror. "Pa...he's here...he's right behind you!" he screamed, his voice high-pitched and frantic.

Arthur froze, his hand tightening around the belt as he turned slowly to look behind him. The moment his eyes landed on the Tall Man; all the color drained from his face. He let out a strangled gasp, his body going rigid with fear.

The belt slipped from his fingers, falling to the floor with a soft thud. Arthur staggered back, clutching his chest, his breath coming in short, labored gasps.

"No...no, it can't be..."

But it was. The Tall Man took a step closer, his twisted smile growing wider, more terrifying. Arthur's knees buckled, and he collapsed to the floor, his hand still gripping his chest as his breath wheezed out in ragged gasps.

"Pa!" Mickey cried, his voice breaking with fear and confusion. He wanted to help his father, to reach out and save him, but he was frozen with terror, his eyes locked on the Tall Man.

Arthur's breath hitched, his body convulsing as he tried to fight the grip of the heart attack that was overtaking him. But his eyes never left the Tall Man, never left that horrifying smile. His mouth opened in a silent scream as his heart gave out, his body going limp on the floor. His son had been right all along. His poor boy. He'd never been good to him. He knew that now. He stared up into the horrible white face with the oversized smile.

That would be the last thing he saw.

Mickey stared in horror, unable to move, unable to breathe. His father was dead—gone, just like Tonya, just like Cherry. And the Tall Man was still there, still smiling, still watching and waiting.

And then, as if in slow motion, The Tall Man began to move toward him, his long legs crossing the distance between them with terrifying speed. His hands were outstretched, and Mickey could see the bloody candy in his hands.

"I saved you some, Mick-kee!"

Mickey's paralysis broke, and he let out a scream that tore through the silence of the night. His scream made the Tall Man flutter. Mickey's small feet pounded on the wooden floor as he raced out of the room, out of the house, and into the night.

The Tall Man followed, his footsteps silent and relentless, his smile never wavering.

Mickey's heart pounded in his chest as he tore through the darkened streets, the wind whipping at his tear-streaked face. He didn't know where he was going, only that he had to get away—away from the house, away from the town, away from the Tall Man.

But no matter how fast he ran, Mickey could feel him, could sense him getting closer. The night seemed to close in around him, the shadows stretching out like claws, trying to pull him back.

His breath came in ragged gasps, his legs burning with the effort of running. He could hear the Tall Man's laughter—low and sinister, echoing in the darkness, mocking him.

Mickey's mind raced with panic, with desperation, but there was nowhere to go, nowhere to hide. And then, just as Mickey thought he couldn't run any farther, the ground gave way beneath him. He stumbled, his foot catching on something unseen, and he fell, tumbling into the cold, wet earth.

Somehow, some way, he had fallen into an open grave. How had he gotten here?

The world spun around him as he tried to climb up. He needed to try to keep running, but it was too late.

The Tall Man was there, standing over him, his shadow stretching long and dark over the boy's trembling form.

Mickey screamed again, but the sound was swallowed by the night, by the darkness that surrounded him. The Tall Man's smile grew wider, his bony hand reaching down, closing the distance between them.

He leaped into the grave with the terrified boy, his hands open still. The bloody candy fell to the ground as he reached for Mickey's neck.

And then everything went black.

55

# Chapter Six–Macie

The Harris house was an old, creaky structure, steeped in history and shadows. As I sat in the dimly lit kitchen, the weight of the day's events pressed down on me like a suffocating blanket.

The rain hadn't let up yet but at least the monstrous lightning had ended although thunder continued to rumble in the distance.

The room smelled of aged wood and the faint scent of something metallic—perhaps the lingering fear and despair that had soaked into the walls over the years. The team was in the living room, interviewing the Harris family, but my mind was elsewhere, focused on the strange, unsettling words I had written earlier.

I couldn't shake the feeling that something dark and terrible was lurking just beyond the edges of my consciousness.

What I was experiencing was hard to explain, if anyone bothered to ask. It was times like this that I really missed my sister, Jocelyn. We got one another, there was never any need to explain myself to her.

The familiar sadness from missing her returned but I had to push it to the side and focus on what's next.

The automatic writing I had channeled in the SUV wasn't just random gibberish—it felt like a message, a warning from something or someone long gone. But the words made no sense to me, a twisted tangle of unfamiliar letters and symbols that had poured out of me like a fever dream. I stared at the words again. I began spelling the words out but they still made no sense to me.

Jericho sat across from me at the worn dining table, his face illuminated by the pale glow of the tablet in front of him. He was focused, his brow furrowed as he scanned the notes I had taken of the writing.

"We need to figure out what these words means," he said quietly, his voice low and serious. "This could be a clue, something that ties everything together."

I nodded, though my hands trembled slightly as I opened my own tablet, pulling up the images of the pages I had filled with the mysterious script. The writing was jagged, almost violent in its intensity, as if whatever had guided my hand was in a frenzy.

It wasn't English—of that I was certain. But what was it? Not French.

The room around us seemed to grow darker, the corners filling with shadows that danced just out of sight, as if they were alive. My skin prickled with the awareness that we were not alone in this house, that the spirits we were dealing with were far from at peace.

"It's not Latin, or any of the other usual languages we come across," Jericho murmured, his eyes scanning the text with a mix of frustration and determination. "There's something about it though...like I've seen it before."

I nodded again, more out of habit than understanding. My mind was racing, trying to make sense of the nonsensical. Then, as the translation software began to spit out the results, a chill ran down my spine. The words...they were starting to make sense.

"It's German," I whispered, more to myself than to Jericho. "The writing...it's in German."

Jericho looked up, his eyes narrowing. "German? Are you sure?"

I nodded, the eerie realization settling in my bones like ice. "Yes! I'm sure. The words are fragmented, but it's definitely German. I don't speak it, but some of these words...they're warnings, Jericho. Warnings about something dark. Something evil."

He leaned closer, peering at the translation on my screen. "What kind of warnings?"

I hesitated, my fingers trembling over the tablet. "It's hard to say. But from what I can make out...there's something about a 'shadow'...and 'children.' And...'him.' We need better translation software."

Jericho's face paled, and he sat back, his gaze turning to the darkened windows. The storm outside had subsided, but the air in the house was thick with a tension that made it hard to breathe.

"The Tall Man," he muttered, more to himself than to me. "This message is from him."

I swallowed hard, the dread coiling in my stomach like a snake. "No way. The writing...it's a warning about him. About what he's done...what he's going to do. Or what he wants to do."

The words hung in the air between us, heavy and foreboding. The German phrases on the screen seemed to pulse with a life of their own, as if they were a living, breathing entity, trying to communicate with us through the veil of time and death.

"We need to tell Midas," Jericho said finally, his voice steady but tinged with fear. "Whatever this is...it's more than just a ghost. It's something far more dangerous."

I nodded my throat too tight to speak. The shadows in the room seemed to grow darker, thicker, as if they were closing in around us, listening to our every word. The house creaked and groaned, the old wood settling, or perhaps something else moving within the walls.

As I stared at the German words on the screen, I couldn't shake the feeling that we were unraveling a mystery far more sinister than we had ever imagined. The Tall Man was out there, watching us, waiting for his moment. And the warnings in the automatic writing were just the beginning.

But what terrified me most was the realization that the shadows in the room—the darkness that seemed to cling to every corner—were not just a figment of my imagination.

They were real.

And they were getting closer.

The shadows in the room felt like they were pressing in on me, suffocating and alive. The realization that the automatic writing was in German—and possibly a warning from the Tall Man or about him—had shaken me to my core. But there was something else gnawing at me, something I couldn't quite put my finger on. The energy in the house felt charged, thick with a tension that made it hard to breathe.

I knew I had to try again, to see if I could reach whatever was trying to communicate with us. I pushed aside my fear and retrieved my notebook, flipping to a fresh page.

Jericho watched me with a mixture of concern and curiosity as I took a deep breath and let the pen hover over the paper.

"Are you sure about this?" he asked, his voice low, almost hesitant. "You've already channeled some pretty dark stuff. Maybe we should wait until we're better prepared."

I shook my head, trying to steady my racing heart. "I have to do this, Jericho. There's something...someone...trying to reach us. And we need to know what they want."

He nodded reluctantly, his eyes never leaving me as I closed my eyes and let my mind go blank, opening myself up to whatever might come through. Almost immediately, I felt the familiar pull, the sensation of something guiding my hand as the pen began to move across the page. I didn't have time to argue with my part time boyfriend.

This time, the writing came faster, more frantic. The words spilled out in a torrent, jagged and harsh, as if whoever—or whatever—was behind them was desperate to communicate. The energy around me crackled, and I could feel the hair on the back of my neck stand on end.

When I finally stopped, my hand trembling, I opened my eyes and looked down at the page. The words were scrawled in a messy, almost illegible script, but the message was clear enough to send a chill down my spine.

*"Help us, he won't let us go."*

Jericho leaned in, reading the words over my shoulder. His face paled, and he swallowed hard. "This is different," he muttered, more to himself than to me.

I nodded my throat was so dry. "It feels different, too. The energy...it's not like before. This isn't just any spirit, Jericho. This feels...stronger. This is a collective message from those missing children."

Jericho frowned, his gaze flicking to the dark corners of the room as if expecting to see something lurking there. "We have to keep an open mind, Macie. You could be channeling anyone. It doesn't necessarily mean it's related to the case or the Tall Man."

I stared at him, disbelief washing over me. "Are you serious? That was him earlier, Jericho. I can feel it. He gave the messages in German. It's the same energy I felt in the playground, the same presence. Why won't you trust my instincts on this?"

Jericho met my gaze, his expression conflicted. "I do trust you, Macie. But we must be careful. We can't jump to conclusions without more evidence. We need to stay objective. That's all I'm saying. What? Don't look at me like that. I'm not saying I don't believe you."

Disappointment twisted in my gut.

He didn't get it—he didn't understand how deeply I felt these things. It wasn't just about evidence or objectivity; it was about intuition, about knowing things that couldn't always be explained.

I sighed and looked down at my pen, which had stopped working midway through the writing. I refused to fight with him. "Great, just what I need," I muttered, pulling my book bag onto my lap to search for a new pen.

I rummaged through the clutter of notebooks, charms, and protective crystals, but my fingers brushed against something soft and unexpected. *What the...?*

Frowning, I pulled the object out, and my heart nearly stopped. It was the doll—the old, weathered doll I had found buried in the playground. I stared at it, my breath catching in my throat. "What the hell?"

Jericho looked up, his eyes widening when he saw what I was holding. "Macie, why do you have that? You know better than that." He lowered his voice, presumably because we were getting too loud.

I shook my head, too stunned to speak. The doll's cracked porcelain face seemed to glare up at me, its single, unblinking eye filled with an eerie, lifeless gaze. I had left it in the playground—I was sure of it. But here it was, in my hands, as if it had followed me.

A cold sweat broke out on my forehead, and I felt a wave of nausea wash over me. This wasn't just a coincidence. The doll, the writing, the oppressive energy in the house—it was all connected, all part of something far more sinister than I had imagined.

"Jericho," I whispered, my voice trembling, "I didn't bring this with me. I don't know how it got here. I would never take something from a haunted location. I would never do that. You know that!"

He didn't answer right away, his gaze locked on the doll as if he expected it to move. When he finally spoke, his voice was laced with unease. "We need to figure out what's going on, Macie. And we need to do it fast. This isn't just a haunting...it's something much worse."

I nodded, clutching the doll to my chest as if it could somehow protect me from the darkness that was closing in around us. The room seemed to grow colder, the shadows darker, as if the house itself was watching, waiting.

And deep down, I knew that whatever was happening to us, it was only just the beginning.

The air between Jericho and me grew thick with tension, the unease turning into something sharper, more personal. I couldn't shake the feeling of dread that had settled over me since finding the doll in my bag. My mind raced, trying to make sense of how it had gotten there, but no logical explanation came to mind.

"Is it possible you just shoved it in there? I mean we were running for our lives during that storm."

"No! I didn't put the doll in my bag, Jericho. I swear," I said, my voice rising with the panic I was trying to keep under control. "You've got to believe me."

Jericho shook his head, his expression skeptical. "Macie, things have been crazy today. Maybe you just don't remember doing it. I mean, we really did run for our lives. That was some storm, huh?"

His tone was calm, almost too calm, and it grated on my nerves.

"No, Jericho! I didn't take the doll. I'm not that reckless! I wouldn't risk bringing something like that with us, especially not knowing what we're dealing with. Why do you keep second-guessing me?"

Out of the corner of my eye I could see Sierra giving me the stare down, but I was pissed. So what if I raised my voice. How dare Jericho accuse me of taking the dang doll!

Jericho's eyes flashed with a mix of surprise and frustration. "I'm not second-guessing you. I'm trying to figure this out, just like you are. But you must admit, it's possible you might have—"

"I didn't!" I interrupted, my voice shaking with anger and fear. "Why won't you just trust me on this? I know what I'm doing, Jericho. You don't have to treat me like some novice who doesn't understand the risks. In case you forgot, I'm not a newbie, Jericho!"

The words hung in the air between us, heavy and charged, and I could see the shock and hurt in Jericho's eyes.

For a moment, he just stared at me, his mouth slightly open as if he was trying to find the right words to say.

But instead of responding, Jericho's expression hardened. "Fine," he muttered, his voice low and cold. "I'm done arguing about this."

Without another word, he turned and walked out of the house, leaving me standing there, clutching the doll, my heart pounding in my chest.

I watched him walk away, a mix of anger and disappointment churning in my gut. Why did he have to be so stubborn? So closed off?

Relationships took work, and if he wasn't willing to put in the effort, then what were we even doing?

My thoughts drifted, unbidden, to Chris.

He had always been more open, more understanding. I missed him—missed the way he made me feel, like I was truly seen and valued. But Chris was off-limits now. He was taking a break from the paranormal, from the team, and I had to respect that.

Besides, daydreaming about him wouldn't solve anything. It was just a distraction from the mess I was in now.

I toyed with the idea of calling him, just to hear his voice, to feel a connection to someone who didn't make me feel like I was losing my mind. But I pushed the thought away.

This wasn't the time for wishful thinking. I had to stay focused on the case.

With a heavy sigh, I pulled out my notebook and pen, determined to make sense of the chaos. The doll sat on the seat beside me, its cracked face staring blankly ahead, a reminder of the darkness that seemed to be closing in around us.

I couldn't let Jericho's doubts shake me. I needed to trust my instincts, no matter how strange or unsettling they might be.

I let the pen hover over the page, closing my eyes and allowing myself to slip into that familiar, trance-like state. The shadows in the kitchen seemed to press closer, the air growing colder as I opened myself up to whatever might come through.

Cassidy had entered the kitchen, but her presence didn't disturb me. She went for a glass of water and then sat at the table with me. I appreciated her quiet company.

Almost immediately, the pen began to move, the words flowing out of me in a frantic rush.

I could feel the presence of someone—no, something—desperate to communicate, the energy more frantic and fearful than before.

When I finally opened my eyes, the words on the page sent a shiver down my spine:

*Please, come find me. He's trapped us all!*

My breath caught in my throat as I stared at the message, the words trembling on the page as if they were alive.

*Tonya. The little girl who had vanished all those years ago—she was reaching out to us, begging for help from beyond the veil.*

The doll seemed to glare up at me, its single eye filled with a cold, lifeless accusation. The message was clear—Tonya was lost in the darkness, trapped by the Tall Man, just like all the others. And now, she was pleading with us to save her.

But how could we fight something so powerful, so ancient?

The fear gnawed at me, but I knew I couldn't back down now. Tonya needed us. All those lost children needed us.

I had to find a way to reach her, to free her from the darkness before it was too late.

As if she knew what I was thinking, Cassidy leaned in close and hugged me.

I laid my head on her shoulder and cried. No, it wasn't the professional thing to do but I needed this moment. I needed my sister but she wasn't here. Jocelyn! I lost her too soon. She'd fought the darkness with her last breath. I would do the same.

And I had a feeling that this case might just cost me everything.

Just like Jocelyn. I clutched the worn doll as Cassidy retrieved a paper towel for my tears. I whispered to her what I suspected, what I'd discovered about the two sessions. She hugged me again and promised me that everything would be okay.

"Come in the living room, Macie. You have to hear Sabra's story. The Harris's are back. Don't worry about Jericho. He'll walk it off."

I wasn't worried about Jericho at all. In fact, I made a decision. One that I'd been putting off for a long time.

I would walk these dark paths alone if I had to, but I was glad to be a part of the team.

But Jericho? We were over. We were too different, with our gifts, with our expectations from one another.

Maybe he loved me. Maybe he didn't, but one thing was for sure, I didn't love him.

Not the way he wanted me to and I was done pretending.

Done with everything.

# Chapter Seven—Sierra

I sat across from Sabra, my eyes scanning her pale face, taking in the way her hands fidgeted nervously in her lap. A pretty girl but she suffered from the same thing most teenage girls suffer from, a lack of self-confidence. Her mom, although understandably stressed out, wasn't making things easy. Interviewing the child without her mother would be ideal but Susan wasn't going to let that happen. I can't say I blame her.

If this had been Emily, I'd be freaking out too.

The rain outside had finally slowed to a drizzle, leaving behind a somber, heavy stillness in the air. The house itself seemed to hold its breath, as if it knew what was coming, and was waiting for the words to spill out.

I could tell Sabra was scared—terrified, actually. I could see it in the way her blue eyes kept darting to her mother, Susan, who stood near the doorway, her lips pressed into a thin, worried line. But I needed to hear from Sabra herself.

Whatever had happened, whatever she and her friend had done, we needed to know the details if we were going to help her. In order to undo what had been done, I needed all the specifics. Without that, we'd be grasping at straws.

Sabra's voice was small, almost a whisper, as she began to speak. "Felicia and I...we didn't mean for any of this to happen. You have to believe me. We just thought...it would be fun, you know? Like the stories you hear about people talking to ghosts. We saw it on television and thought it would be cool."

My heart sank a little as I listened. I'd heard too many stories like this before, and they never ended well. Kids playing with things they didn't understand, thinking it was all a game, until it wasn't.

"It's okay. You were curious. I get it. What did you do, Sabra? How did you use the board?" I asked, keeping my voice as calm as possible, though my mind was racing.

She nodded, her eyes widening with the memory. "Um, well, we, uh…"

Susan appeared to become frustrated with her daughter. She wasn't helping the situation. "Just tell them, Sabra. I'm not mad at you, but you have to be honest."

Sabra pressed her pink lips together and closed her eyes for a moment as if she were steadying herself before taking a leap off a building.

*Why in God's name did I think that?*

I glanced at Macie and was grateful that she could not read my mind.

"We did it late at night when no one else was around. Felicia's mom was working late, Mom had something at work, and we thought it would be cool to try and talk to…whoever was out there. Even before the board though, my room was creepy. It was creepy then and now it is creepier."

I leaned in closer, feeling the gravity of the situation settle over me like a weight. "And what happened when you used it? Did you make contact? Did you use any special utterances? Any games? Did you both put your hands on the planchette?"

Sabra swallowed hard, glancing at her mother again before looking back at me. "No utterances, whatever that is. You mean like spells?"

I nodded patiently. "I don't know any but we didn't use any magic words. We just followed the directions in the game. We both put our fingers on the planchette. At first, nothing happened. But then the planchette started moving on its own, spelling out words. It wasn't scary at first, just names and stuff. But the more we used it, then it got weird…like it knew things about us, things we hadn't told anyone."

My stomach twisted into a knot. "Sabra, has anyone spoken to Felicia? Is she okay?" I asked, my voice gaining an edge of urgency. If the entity had latched onto Sabra, there was no telling what it might have done to Felicia. "If it knows about you, it knows about her."

Sabra's lower lip trembled, and I could see the tears welling up in her eyes. "I...I don't know. I haven't talked to her since everything started happening. Mom says we can't be friends anymore because she's trouble, but I'm scared for her. What if it's going after her, too? Mom, please. Let me text her. I need my phone back."

Her fear was palpable, and I knew we had to act fast. This was more than just a simple haunting—this was something darker, something that had the potential to do real harm.

"You're not getting that phone back, Sabra. I'm not going to lose you again!"

I was determined not to get in the middle of this argument and so far, the rest of the team had kept themselves busy investigating upstairs. Except for Jericho who was pouting in the SUV.

Honestly, these two were made for one another. Both Jericho and Macie had plenty of angst on their own. Together they were triple angsty, like two teenagers.

"What exactly did the board say to you? And did it mention Felicia at all? Did it threaten you?"

Sabra began to cry. The words hung in the air between us, heavy with the knowledge that whatever had been unleashed was far from finished with Sabra—or Felicia.

"It said it would eat us. It would eat us and suck on our bones. That freaked me out so bad I didn't want to continue. Felicia kept going though. She got mad at it and yelled at it. She was fearless but I knew she was wrong. She was doing wrong but I couldn't stop her. We got in an argument; she left and slammed the door but then I was alone with the board. I slid it under the bed and tried to figure out what to do."

Susan pulled out her phone with trembling hands. I could see the anxiety etched on her face, her fingers shaking as she dialed Felicia's mother. Sabra watched her mother intently, her eyes wide with a mixture of fear and guilt, while I leaned back slightly, giving them space but still listening closely.

My mind raced with possibilities—none of them good. If this entity had latched onto Sabra, it could easily have set its sights on Felicia as well.

"Hi, Grace, it's Susan," she began, her voice thin and strained. She paused, listening, her face growing paler by the second. "Yes, she's fine. Staying home and I'm keeping her close. I'm calling to check on Felicia. Have you noticed anything strange lately? Is she okay?"

I could only hear Susan's side of the conversation, but I saw the color drain from her face as Grace responded. My pulse quickened, a cold chill creeping up my spine.

"She's where?" Susan asked, her voice tight with disbelief. "Out of town? Why?"

I could tell from Susan's expression that this wasn't good news. Her gaze flicked over to me, her eyes wide with a sudden, raw fear. "Grace sent Felicia to live with her father," she said after a moment, covering the phone with her hand. "She's been missing school, acting out. Grace thought it would be better for her to get away for a while."

My blood ran cold. "Did she say when Felicia left?" I asked, my voice low but urgent.

"A few days ago. Just after...everything started happening," Susan replied, her voice trembling. She relayed the message to Grace, thanking her before ending the call. I could see the panic building in her eyes, and I felt it too—Felicia might be miles away, but that didn't mean she was safe.

Susan hung up the phone and turned to Sabra, her fear morphing into a flash of anger.

"This is your fault, Sabra! Do you see what you've done? This isn't a game! You could have put your friend in serious danger!" I couldn't believe what I was hearing.

Sabra's eyes filled with tears, her hands trembling as she tried to defend herself. "Mom, I didn't mean to! I didn't skip school, I swear! All I did was play with the board. It wasn't even my idea! Felicia said it would be fun, but I didn't know—"

"Fun? Fun?" Susan's voice rose, her frustration bubbling over. "You're grounded for...I can't even think of how long! You're not getting that phone back, not after this. Ever!"

"But Dad calls me on that phone! Mom! You can't keep my phone. I need to talk to Dad!"

I could feel the tension escalating, and I knew I had to step in before it spiraled out of control. "Susan, where's the board now?" I asked, keeping my voice as calm and steady as possible.

Susan shot me a bewildered look. "I threw it away," she said, almost dismissively. "It's gone, taken out with the garbage."

My heart sank. That's right. She said that earlier, but I was hoping we would be able to retrieve and banish it properly. "You threw it away? When?"

"A few days ago," she replied, her tone still sharp. "Why does it matter?"

I felt a wave of dread wash over me. "Because the board needs to be closed properly, Susan. It's not just about getting rid of it. If it's still active, it could be keeping a portal open giving whatever this is direct access to Sabra and probably Felicia too."

The room fell silent, the gravity of my words hanging in the air like a dark cloud. Susan and Sabra glanced at Midas who backed me up with a nod of his head.

I could see the realization dawning on Susan, her eyes widening with horror. Sabra, still on the verge of tears, looked at me, her expression pleading.

"What do we do now?" Susan whispered, her voice barely audible, as though saying it louder would make it even more real. "How do I protect my daughter? Do we have to move too?"

"We need to find a way to close that portal," I said, my voice firm despite the fear gnawing at my insides. "We'll do everything we can, but we need to act fast. The longer it stays open, the more dangerous this situation becomes."

The air in the room seemed to grow heavier, the silence thick with fear and uncertainty.

We were facing something far more sinister than I had initially thought, and the fact that the board was gone made it even more terrifying.

"We have to close that door," I repeated, more to myself than to them, as the weight of what lay ahead settled over me like a shroud.

I could see the panic rising in Susan's eyes, her breath coming in quick, shallow gasps as the gravity of the situation sank in. The board, tossed away like yesterday's trash, was now a ticking time bomb, a gateway that could unleash horrors far beyond anything this family had ever imagined.

Susan's reaction was immediate and visceral. Her hand flew to her mouth, her eyes wide with terror as she began to hyperventilate. "What do you mean? He's already in this house, isn't he? He's going to come for her!"

Her voice was rising in pitch, verging on hysteria, and I could see Sabra shrinking back, her own fear feeding off her mother's.

I reached out to Susan, trying to steady her, but she was too far gone, her panic taking over.

Midas stepped in, his presence a calming force in the midst of the chaos. He placed a firm hand on Susan's shoulder, guiding her to sit down. "Susan, listen to me," he said, his voice low and reassuring. "We're not going to let anything happen to Sabra. We will find a way to close that portal, even without the physical board. But we need you to stay calm. We can't do this without your help. Sabra needs you, we need you. Let's focus on the solution."

Susan's eyes were wide with fear, but she nodded, her breathing gradually slowing as she clung to Midas's words like a lifeline. I could see the struggle in her eyes, the desperate need to believe that everything would be okay. But I knew, deep down, that this was far from over.

Midas glanced at me, his expression serious but calm. "We'll find a way," he repeated, his eyes locking onto mine, and I nodded, though my heart was pounding. The truth was, the task had just become infinitely more dangerous, and we were venturing into uncharted territory without a map.

Just as the situation began to calm down, Cassidy, who had been quietly flipping through her notebook, suddenly looked up, her expression one of dawning realization.

"Guys, did you know that this is the same house where Cherry Adams was found in 1902?"

Her words hit like a punch to the gut, the room falling into an eerie silence as the implication sank in. I felt a chill run down my spine, the pieces of the puzzle beginning to fall into place in a way that made my blood run cold.

Cassidy looked around at us, her eyes wide. "It might not be the board at all. It might be the location. Or a combination of them both."

The revelation hung in the air like a dark cloud, the weight of it pressing down on us. I could feel the atmosphere in the room shift, the sense of impending doom growing stronger. If this house had been harboring something dark for over a century, then the board might have only been a catalyst, a trigger for something much more ancient and malevolent.

"This place...this entity...it's been here all along," I murmured, the realization sending a fresh wave of dread through me. "The board may have just woken it up."

The room seemed to close in around us, the walls pressing in with the weight of history that had seeped into the very foundations of this house. We were dealing with something far more sinister than we had initially thought, and the stakes had just been raised exponentially.

"We need to dig deeper," Midas said, his voice firm. "Find out everything we can about this house, this area. Let's confirm what we suspect. There's more to this than we realized, and if we're going to help y'all, we need to understand exactly what we're dealing with."

I nodded, my mind racing as I considered the possibilities.

The board, the house, the history of Cherry Adams—all of it was connected, woven together in a web of darkness that we were only just beginning to unravel. And somewhere in that darkness, the entity was waiting, watching, biding its time.

But we would be ready. We had to be.

# Chapter Eight–Sierra

Dusk settled over Dead Children's Playground like a shroud, the last remnants of daylight slipping away, leaving behind a world cloaked in shadow. I was strangely nauseated and exhausted.

*Geesh. I hope I'm not coming down with something.*

But I also had that strange metallic sensation in my mouth. No, these weren't my feelings I was experiencing. This was the empathic part of my psychic gift—I was picking up on someone else's feelings. Someone was sick. I glanced around at the crew but nobody appeared ill.

The playground, which had seemed so ordinary in the harsh light of day, now transformed into something otherworldly, a place where the veil between the living and the dead felt paper-thin.

The swings moved gently in the breeze, creaking like old bones, while the slide stood as a silent sentinel, watching, waiting. Such a fine playground, well kept, obviously lovingly designed and created, but still creepy.

The air was thick with the scent of earth, damp and heavy, mingled with something sharper—something metallic that clung to the back of my throat, making it hard to swallow.

I breathed in, and the smell reminded me of blood, fresh and pungent, though I knew it was just my imagination. Or at least, I hoped it was.

We had returned to the playground with a singular goal—to find where the children's bodies were hidden, to give them the peace they had been denied for so long. But as I stepped onto the soft ground, I couldn't shake the feeling that we were being watched, that countless eyes, unseen and accusing, were fixed on us from the darkness.

The trees surrounding the playground loomed like dark giants, their branches reaching out like skeletal fingers, blocking out what little light remained.

A chill ran down my spine as I imagined the spirits of the children—lost, scared, and alone—trapped here in the shadows, waiting for someone to find them, to set them free.

I closed my eyes and did my best to sense their sweet spirits, but I got nothing.

I noticed Midas was strangely quiet.

I glanced at the others, seeing the same unease mirrored in their faces. Macie clutched her notebook to her chest, her eyes wide as she scanned the playground, searching for any sign of movement.

Jericho and Joshua were setting up the equipment, their expressions tense, their movements precise and methodical, as if the routine could somehow ward off the fear that gnawed at the edges of our minds.

Cassidy already had her sketchbook out but she was staring out into space. I knew that look.

*Good! At least one of us has got a bead on something.*

The wind picked up, rustling the leaves and sending a shiver through me. I wrapped my arms around myself, trying to ward off the cold that had nothing to do with the temperature.

The silence was oppressive, broken only by the occasional creak of the swings and the distant rustle of the leaves, like whispered secrets carried on the wind.

"This place is...different at night," Jericho murmured, his voice low, almost reverent, as if he were afraid to disturb the ghosts that lingered here. "I say we set up equipment here in the playground, but we go into the cemetery too."

I nodded as my throat tightened. "We need to find them," I said, my voice barely above a whisper. "We need to find where they're buried, where he hid them." My desperation was rising and I couldn't explain this strange bombardment of anxiety and sadness I was experiencing. This was not my first rodeo. I knew how to keep my feelings in check.

The ground beneath my feet felt soft, almost spongy from the rain earlier. It was as if it were hiding something just beneath the surface. I swallowed hard, pushing away the rising panic that threatened to choke me.

We had to keep going. We had to uncover the truth, no matter how terrifying it might be.

Macie knelt on the ground, her notebook open on her lap, and I could see the tension in her shoulders as she prepared to connect with the spirits trapped in this forsaken place. I noticed she had the doll with her. She set it against the rock structure that lined one side of the playground. Jericho was shaking his head disapprovingly, but he didn't say a word.

What was he so worried about? The doll wasn't the cause of the haunting. Just an unfortunate object left behind. I touched it earlier. It harbored no secrets. It was just an empty vessel, a thrown away toy.

The last light of day had faded completely, leaving us in near darkness, save for the dim glow of our flashlights. The air around us seemed to grow colder, heavier, as if the night itself were pressing down on us, suffocating us.

"I'm going to try to reach them," Macie said, her voice trembling slightly. "This had to have belonged to one of the children." She took a deep breath, her hand hovering over the pen as she closed her eyes and opened her mind to whatever might be lingering here. I watched as she began to write, her hand moving slowly at first, then faster, as if guided by an unseen force.

"Please," she whispered, her voice soft, pleading. "We want to help you. Tell us where you are. We want to give you peace."

For a moment, everything seemed still, the only sound the scratch of Macie's pen against the paper.

But then, something shifted.

*Oh no! Jericho was right! This is a bad idea! Automatic writing in the cemetery is always a bad idea!*

The energy around us grew darker, more oppressive, and I could see the strain on Macie's face as the pen began to move more violently across the page.

"Macie, let's wait, huh?" I asked as I made my way to her.

Her writing grew jagged, harsh, the lines slashing across the paper as if driven by anger, by fear. The words that formed were not in English, not anymore. They were in German again, dark and twisted, the letters barely legible, scrawled in a frenzied hand.

Macie gasped, her eyes flying open as she threw the pen down, as if it had burned her.

"No," she whispered, her voice filled with fear. "No, I don't want to hear this. I don't want to see it. I'm not going to write it!"

The air around us seemed to thicken, the cold pressing in from all sides, making it hard to breathe. I could feel the darkness closing in, the malevolent presence that had taken hold of this place growing stronger, feeding off our fear.

Midas touched my shoulder, I nearly jumped three feet off the ground.

"Hey, Little Sister. Take a few deep breaths." I slapped on a smile and set about digging for my digital recorder. Why did I feel so terrified? This wasn't like me at all.

Jericho returned, stepping into the circle of light cast by our flashlights. He said nothing, just watched Macie with a look of deep concern. At least she'd stopped writing.

The silence between them was heavy, charged with unspoken words, with the weight of what she had just experienced.

I could feel it too—the oppressive energy, the sense that we were being watched, hunted.

The night was alive with this bad energy, the darkness was filled with whispers, with the echo of the children's cries, and the laughter of something far more sinister. I wanted to cover my ears and scream the noises all away.

We were in over our heads, and we all knew it. But there was no turning back now.

We had to keep going, had to find a way to bring light to this darkness, before it consumed us all.

As we decided to move deeper into the Maple Hill Cemetery, the air grew colder and heavier with the weight of the past.

The fading light of dusk cast long, twisted shadows across the ground, making the headstones look like jagged teeth rising from the earth.

The wind whispered through the trees, carrying with it a faint, mournful sound, as if the spirits buried here were trying to warn us of the darkness that lingered. That it was about to pounce at any moment.

We wandered into a more secluded section of the cemetery, a place where the gravestones were older, more weather-worn, their inscriptions barely legible beneath layers of moss and time. But as we walked, I noticed a pattern—many of the names etched into the stones were German.

My breath caught in my throat as I read them aloud, my fingers tracing the cold stone, each name sending a shiver down my spine.

"Johann, Gertrude, Wilhelm..." I murmured, the names heavy on my tongue, each one more foreign and unfamiliar than the last.

The fog began to creep in, swirling around our feet like the breath of the dead, chilling us to the bone. I could feel the presence of something ancient and malevolent, something that had been here long before we arrived, and would remain long after we were gone.

The air was thick with it, suffocating in its intensity, and I could sense that we were not welcome here.

"This place...there's something wrong here," Cassidy whispered, her voice trembling as she stared at the gravestones. "It's like they're watching us."

I nodded, my heart pounding in my chest. "These names...they're all German and they're old, really old. This section of the cemetery...it feels different, like it's hiding something. We're on the right track, I think. Macie, walk with me."

"Okay," she said as she slung her backpack up on her shoulder. She skipped a step to join me. I could see she was eager to avoid Jericho. Yeah, that was a problem.

As we continued walking, I felt a strange pull, as if something—or someone—was guiding me, drawing me towards a specific grave. My fingers tingled as I reached out, my pulse quickening as I read the name etched into the stone.

"Heinrich Thornton." A cold sweat broke out on my forehead, and I felt a wave of nausea wash over me. I touched his gravestone and was immediately filled with dread. I snatched my hand away as the picture of an abyss filled my mind. And in it, was a monster, tall and thin, climbing up. Ready to pounce.

"Guys...this is it. This is him," I said, my voice barely above a whisper. "Heinrich Thornton...this is the Tall Man. Or at least, who he used to be."

The fog thickened around us, swirling like a living thing, as if the cemetery itself was reacting to our presence.

The idea that the Tall Man might have once been human, with his own tragic story, began to take hold, and I felt a deep, gnawing dread settle in the pit of my stomach.

I knew, without a doubt, that we had found the source of the darkness that had taken hold of this place. Still had to prove that though but I had no doubt I was right. I knew I needed to trust my intuition and I did.

My hand trembled as I rested it again on Heinrich Thornton's gravestone, the cold stone sending a shiver up my arm.

The moment my fingers made contact a second time, a shock of energy jolted through me, like a lightning bolt shooting up my spine. I gasped, my vision blurring as a rush of images flashed before my eyes—fragments of memories, scenes from a life long past, twisted and dark.

I saw children, their faces pale and frightened, crying out for help as they were dragged into the shadows.

I could feel their terror, their desperation, as they were trapped, bound to this cursed land by Thornton's twisted will. The visions were so vivid, so overwhelming, that I could barely breathe, the weight of their fear crushing me.

I stumbled back, tearing my hand away from the gravestone as if it had burned me.

My heart pounded in my chest, my breath coming in short, panicked gasps as I tried to shake off the lingering remnants of the vision. But the images stayed with me, burned into my mind, and I knew that what I had seen was the truth.

"He's here," I whispered, my voice shaking. "He's still here, trapping them, feeding off their fear to maintain his power. The Tall Man...he's Heinrich Thornton. He's not just a ghost...he's something much worse. He's no longer human! Not human!"

The oppressive energy swirled around us, thick and suffocating, as if the very air was trying to crush us. I could feel Thornton's presence, his malevolence radiating from the grave, seeping into the ground, into the playground, into the children's spirits that he had claimed.

"We need to leave," I said, my voice barely audible, but filled with a sense of urgency. "Now. Before he tries to trap us too. We're not ready, guys! Not ready!"

But even as I spoke, I knew that leaving wouldn't be enough. Thornton's spirit was strong, anchored to this place by the darkness he had created, and he wouldn't let us go easily.

We were in his domain now, and he would do everything in his power to keep us here.

As we turned to leave, I felt a cold hand brush against my shoulder, sending a jolt of fear through me. I spun around, but there was nothing there—just the fog, thick and impenetrable, hiding whatever lurked in the darkness.

But I knew he was there, watching, waiting. And I knew, deep down, that this was far from over.

The air grew colder, the chill cutting through my jacket and sending a shiver down my spine. The fog thickened, swirling around us like a living thing, and with it came a deep sense of dread.

It felt as if the cemetery itself was waking up, the dead stirring beneath the earth, aware of our presence.

A rustling sound echoed through the trees, followed by the faintest whisper, like someone—or something—was speaking just out of earshot. I strained to listen, but the words were lost in the wind, a hissing, unintelligible murmur that seemed to come from all directions at once.

The shadows, which had been still moments ago, began to stretch and twist, taking on shapes that darted in and out of sight. Figures loomed in the corner of my vision, only to vanish the moment I turned to face them. My pulse quickened, each beat thudding in my ears as panic clawed at the edges of my mind.

Suddenly, Joshua's hand was in mine. I was never so grateful to have his hand in mine.

The others felt it too. Macie's breath came in quick, shallow gasps, her eyes wide with fear as she clutched her notebook to her chest. Jericho's flashlight flickered, the beam weak and wavering, until it sputtered out completely, plunging us into near darkness.

"Midas," I whispered, my voice trembling. "Something's not right. We need to get out of here."

Our fearless leader didn't respond immediately, his eyes scanning the cemetery, searching for something—anything—that might explain the sudden change in atmosphere. But all he found were more shadows, more whispers, more unseen presences that seemed to close in around us.

"I feel it too," he finally said, his voice tight with tension. "Everyone, stay close. Sierra is right. We're leaving but we stick together."

As if on cue, I felt something brushing against my shoulder—a cold, clammy hand that sent a jolt of terror through me. I spun around, my flashlight sweeping through the fog, but there was nothing there. Just the darkness, thick and impenetrable, hiding whatever lurked within.

"Did you feel that?" I gasped, my heart racing. "Something touched me!" Why was I freaking out over a mere touch? Now I was terrified and I wanted to vomit. "God, I feel so sick!"

The others exchanged frightened glances; their own fear mirrored in my eyes. The cemetery seemed to come alive around us, the ground beneath our feet shifting as if it were trying to swallow us whole. The rustling leaves grew louder, the whispers more insistent, until it felt like the very air was pressing in on us, suffocating us.

"We need to move. Now!" Midas ordered, his voice cutting through the panic that threatened to overwhelm us.

We didn't need to be told twice. We scrambled out of the cemetery, our footsteps quick and uneven as we made our way back to the SUV.

The fog followed us, thick and relentless, as if it were trying to pull us back into the darkness.

By the time we reached the vehicle, we were all breathing hard, our nerves frayed and our bodies trembling. The cemetery loomed behind us, a dark, foreboding presence that seemed to watch us as we fled.

Midas slid into the driver's seat, his hands gripping the steering wheel tightly. He didn't say a word as he started the engine, his face pale and drawn. None of us spoke as we drove back to the hotel, the silence heavy with the weight of what we had just experienced.

The darkness pressed in on us from all sides, and I couldn't shake the feeling that we had narrowly escaped something far worse than we could have imagined.

The cemetery had come alive, and whatever lurked within it wasn't done with us yet.

Back at the hotel, the tension hadn't eased. If anything, it had only grown worse, the fear from the cemetery clinging to us like a second skin. We huddled outside our rooms, trying to encourage one another. After some poor attempts at levity, we all departed to our own rooms.

I noticed that Macie didn't go in the room with Jericho. She was talking to him and it didn't look like a good conversation. I sure didn't want to get involved. I tapped Joshua on the shoulder, and he slid the card key in the slot.

Joshua and I sat on the edge of the bed, the silence between us thick with unspoken dread. I pulled out my laptop, my hands still trembling as I typed "Heinrich Thornton" into the search bar. The screen glowed in the dim light, casting long shadows on the walls, shadows that seemed to move and shift as if they had a life of their own.

The search results were sparse, but eventually, I found what I was looking for—an old, grainy photograph of Heinrich Thornton, taken sometime in the late 1800s. My breath caught in my throat as I stared at the image, my blood running cold.

The man in the picture had the same eerie smile as the Tall Man, his eyes dark and hollow, as if they had seen too much, lived too long. His face was gaunt, almost skeletal, with high cheekbones and thin lips that curled into a smirk that sent a shiver down my spine.

"This is him," I whispered, my voice barely audible. "Heinrich Thornton...he is the Tall Man. He was an evil man in life, but he wasn't always evil. Bad things happened to him, those horrible deeds made him become something else. In death, he took on this persona. I don't think there's any humanity left in him."

Joshua leaned in, his eyes narrowing as he studied the photograph. "He looks...wrong," he muttered, his voice tinged with unease. "There's something off about him. Something evil. Although, to be fair, these old photos don't flatter anyone, do they?"

I nodded, swallowing hard as I clicked on the accompanying article. The words on the screen blurred together as I read, my mind racing to piece together the fragments of the story.

"He was a toymaker," I said, my voice trembling as I continued to read. "But he was accused of harming a child—some say he was a monster, that he did...unspeakable things to the children in the town—here in Huntsville. The townspeople found out, and they...they killed him. They dragged him out of his house and beat him to death."

Joshua's face paled as he listened, the horror of the story sinking in. "And now...he's come back. For revenge."

I nodded, my heart pounding in my chest. "He's been trapping the children's spirits, feeding off their fear, keeping them here with him. He's not just a ghost, Joshua...he's something much worse. He's become something...evil."

The pieces of the puzzle were falling into place, but with each revelation, the dread in my stomach grew stronger. Heinrich Thornton's spirit had been twisted by his death, turned into a malevolent force that had been terrorizing this town for over a century.

And now, we had to find a way to stop him.

The darkness outside the window seemed to press in closer, and I couldn't shake the feeling that Heinrich was watching us, waiting for his moment to strike.

We were running out of time, and I knew that if we didn't act fast, we might not make it out of this alive.

# Chapter Nine–Midas

The morning light filtered through the windows of the hotel lobby, casting long shadows across the table where we had gathered. The air was thick with the smell of stale coffee and the lingering tension from the night before.

I could see the exhaustion etched into the faces of my team, but there was something else there too—a steely determination, a resolve to see this through to the end.

We'd all had our fair share of sleepless nights, but this one felt different.

I felt different. I felt tired, burned out actually, but I would not allow myself to consider taking a break. Not when so many people were reaching out for help.

Honestly, the weight of what we were dealing with this case was heavier, more personal. It wasn't just another case; it was a battle against something that had been festering in the shadows for over a century.

Sierra sat at the head of the table, her laptop open in front of her, the glow from the screen casting an eerie light across her face. She was focused, her eyes scanning the documents she'd pulled up, piecing together the final fragments of the puzzle. Her soggy bowl of cereal sat beside her untouched.

"You'll never guess," she said, her voice breaking the silence that had settled over the team. "I mean, even I can't believe it but it is true. The Harris home is Heinrich Thornton's old home. I found the deeds online. He was living in that house. That's where Cherry Adams was found too."

The room seemed to grow colder as her words sank in. People around us glanced at us and we immediately lowered our voices.

"Now we've got Sabra," I whispered as I drank the dregs of my stale coffee. Why was I drinking coffee again?

I glanced around at the others—Macie, Jericho, Cassidy, and Joshua—and saw the same mix of fear and determination mirrored in their eyes. "That is incredibly bad. Good catch, Little Sister. What you're saying is that Heinrich whatever his name is—"

"Heinrich Thornton," she corrected me.

We all knew what this meant. Thornton wasn't just some random ghost terrorizing the town; he was a malevolent force rooted in a place that had witnessed unspeakable horrors.

"What else did you find?" I asked, my voice low, almost hesitant, as if saying the words out loud would make it all too real.

"Like it was mentioned before, Thornton was a toymaker. He owned a shop not far from his house. He got accused of some nasty crimes involving children back in 1892. Some children went missing, others were found dead. Heinrich denied the accusations, but he was arrested and one night, a mob, a lynch mob managed to get their hands on him. They tortured him—good Lord—but he wouldn't confess. He wouldn't tell them where the bodies of the missing children were, so they hung him. Hung him from a tree in the cemetery."

A chill ran down my spine as I stared at the screen, the realization hitting me like a punch to the gut. The house—Thornton's old home—was the epicenter of everything we'd been dealing with. It wasn't just a haunted location; it was the source of the evil that had been plaguing this town for over a century. It was just bad luck that the house sat next to the cemetery and the playground. But I had a worse feeling about the shop.

"We need to go see the shop," I said, my voice steady despite the fear gnawing at my insides. "We need to see it for ourselves and the tree. Any ideas which tree they hung him from?"

"I think we can work that out. Let me take a screenshot with my phone. Ugh. The reflection off the laptop screen. Josh? Can you fix that?" Joshua adjusted the laptop. "That looks great. We'll find it, it's a unique looking tree. That is, if it's still standing," Sierra said sadly as she took another picture.

The others nodded in agreement; their faces grim but resolute. There was no turning back now.

We had to confront Thornton's spirit, to put an end to this nightmare once and for all.

The drive to the old shop was tense, the silence in the SUV broken only by the occasional murmur of conversation and the soft hum of the engine. The town gave way to winding roads and dense woods, the scenery growing more desolate with each passing mile.

The old shop came into view, and my breath caught in my throat.

It was a dilapidated, vine-covered structure, its windows broken, its roof sagging under the weight of years of neglect. But even in its decay, there was something about it that sent a shiver down my spine.

We parked the SUV at the edge of the overgrown driveway, the gravel crunching under the tires as we came to a stop. No one spoke as we got out, the weight of the moment hanging heavy in the air.

The shop loomed before us, silent and foreboding, a monument to the horrors that had unfolded within its walls. The vines that covered it seemed to writhe and twist, as if alive, reaching out like the grasping fingers of the dead. I took a deep breath, trying to steady my nerves.

"This is it," I said, my voice barely above a whisper. "This is where it all began. Keep your eyes open. If anyone asks, we're doing research for a documentary."

I had no idea what kind of research would warrant six investigators but here we were.

My team gathered around me, their faces pale but resolute. We all knew what we had to do, but that didn't make it any easier. The air was thick with the scent of decay, the oppressive feeling of Thornton's presence pressing down on us like a physical weight.

"We go in together," I said, glancing at each of them in turn. "No one goes off on their own. We stick together, no matter what happens."

They nodded, their eyes filled with determination, but I could see the fear lurking just beneath the surface. We were about to walk into the heart of darkness, and none of us knew what we would find. But we had come too far to turn back now. We had to face whatever was waiting for us inside that building to confront the evil that had taken root there, and to put an end to it once and for all.

It wasn't like me to trespass, but this situation called for unusual measures. A faded sign hung outside but the writing was too faded to read. The buildings on either side of the old shop were in just as bad a shape.

As we approached the front door, the cold seeped into my bones, and the weight of what we were about to do settled over me like a shroud.

The door creaked open, the sound echoing through the silence like a death knell.

"Looks, like we were expected," Joshua said ruefully.

"Believe that," Jericho added. "We are being watched, guys."

And with that, we stepped into the darkness.

The floor creaked and groaned beneath us as we moved cautiously through the decaying rooms, each step echoing with the weight of the past. The walls were lined with peeling wallpaper, the once-vibrant patterns now faded and discolored, like the memories that had seeped into the very fabric of this place.

The air was thick with dust and the smell of mildew, a scent that clung to the back of my throat, making each breath feel heavy.

I could feel Cassidy close behind me, her footsteps soft but deliberate as we navigated the messy place. Something ran across the floor and she yelped before laughing at herself. It was only a mouse but if there was one, there were plenty more.

The oppressive energy we'd felt outside was even stronger here, pressing down on us like an invisible force, making it hard to think, hard to breathe. Hard to be living.

*Wow. That's a strange thought.*

"This place is a time capsule—a weird relic," Cassidy whispered, her voice barely audible over the creaking floorboards. "It's like stepping back in time. How is it that after all this time, nobody has done anything with this place. There are even springs and doll parts here and there." She squatted down and shuffled through a wooden box.

"Be careful," I reminded her. "Your furry friend might have friends of his own." She quickly withdrew her hand.

I nodded, though I couldn't shake the feeling that we weren't alone. Joshua was right about that.

The crumbling shop seemed to pulse with a life of its own, the shadows shifting and twisting as if something was watching us, waiting for the right moment to reveal itself.

We entered what must have once been a sitting room, the remnants of old furniture scattered about, covered in layers of dust and cobwebs.

A fireplace, long cold and unused, stood as a silent witness to the horrors that had played out within these walls. The air felt colder here, more oppressive, and I couldn't help but shudder as we stepped further into the room.

Cassidy was the first to notice the oddity in the floorboards—a slight unevenness that caught her eye. She knelt down, her fingers brushing over the wood, and I could see the spark of curiosity in her eyes.

"There's something here," she murmured, her voice tinged with both excitement and dread. She tugged at the floorboard, and with a groan, it gave way, revealing a small, hidden compartment beneath.

My heart raced as I crouched down beside her, peering into the dark space.

Inside, nestled in the dust and debris, were several old, leather-bound diaries, their covers worn and cracked with age. Cassidy carefully lifted one out, the leather soft and fragile in her hands.

"These must have belonged to Thornton," she said, her voice barely above a whisper as she opened the first diary. The pages were yellowed and brittle, the ink faded but still legible.

I leaned closer, my eyes scanning the first few lines. The handwriting was cramped and uneven, the words spilling out in a frantic, almost desperate scrawl.

As Cassidy turned the pages, we began to try and piece together the twisted narrative of Heinrich Thornton's mind—a mind consumed by obsession and madness. He wrote in German, so we were constantly having to use Sierra's translation app.

The entries started innocuously enough, detailing the mundane aspects of Thornton's life—a toymaker by trade, living alone in this house on the outskirts of town. But as we read on, the tone shifted, growing darker, more erratic.

We couldn't catch all the details with just a phone and fading light. We needed to dig deeper, do more research before we came for this guy.

"They're like angels," one entry read. "Pure, untouched by the darkness of this world. I must protect them, keep them safe from harm. The townspeople don't understand—they never will."

My stomach twisted as we continued reading, the words on the pages becoming more and more disturbing.

As Thornton's obsession with certain children grew, his entries became more frantic, more disconnected from reality. He wrote of his anger towards the townspeople, how they had turned against him, accusing him of terrible things.

"These people don't see it—they don't understand the magic of children," another entry read. "They don't treasure them. The children need me. They're lost, abandoned by the world. I'm the only one who can save them."

Cassidy's hands shook as she turned the pages, her breath coming in short, sharp gasps. "He was a mad man." I could see the horror in her eyes as the full extent of Thornton's madness became clear.

He had believed the children were his to protect, to keep safe, even if it meant trapping their spirits in the shop, his house, in the playground, forever.

"This isn't just a haunting," Cassidy whispered, her voice trembling. "He's keeping them as prisoners. He's still here, Midas. He's still trying to protect them, in his own twisted way, but he's not."

I felt a cold shiver run down my spine as the truth settled over us like a suffocating blanket. I placed my hand on my wife's shoulder and felt her trembling.

Thornton's spirit had not moved on—it was still here, still clinging to the creepy obsession that had consumed him in life. He wasn't just haunting this town; he was holding the children's spirits captive, feeding off their fear, their innocence. But clearly he needed new victims, living victims with lots of bright, shiny souls.

As Sierra read on, the final entries in the diary grew more erratic, more desperate.

Thornton's handwriting became almost illegible, the words scrawled across the pages in a frenzy of emotion.

"They're mine," one entry read, the ink smudged as if written in a trembling hand. "They belong to me. The townspeople will never take them from me. I'll protect them, even in death. I'll keep them safe, forever."

I felt a wave of nausea wash over me as I closed the diary, my hands trembling. The weight of what we had uncovered was almost too much to bear. Thornton's twisted sense of companionship had led him to trap these innocent souls, to bind them to this place in a desperate attempt to protect them from a world he saw as cruel and unforgiving.

"He's not going to let them go," I said, my voice barely above a whisper. "Not without a fight." Cassidy looked at me, her eyes wide with fear, but there was a determination there too—a resolve to see this through, no matter what it took.

"We have to find a way to stop him," she said, her voice steady despite the fear that lingered in the air. "We have to free these children and stop him from taking more."

I nodded, the weight of the diaries heavy in my hands. We had uncovered the truth, but the battle was far from over. Thornton's spirit was still hovering here, still holding the children captive in his twisted sense of protection.

And it was up to us to put an end to it, once and for all.

My breath came in shallow gasps as I tried to process the full horror of what we'd uncovered. The room seemed to close in on us, the walls pressing tighter, the darkness growing thicker with each passing second.

My breath puffed out in front of me in a thin, white mist, and a shiver ran down my spine as the cold seeped into my bones.

Something was here with us—something malevolent, something angry.

Cassidy's eyes widened as she clutched one of the diaries to her chest, her knuckles white with fear. The air around us seemed to thicken, growing dense and oppressive, as if we were being smothered by an unseen force.

The sound of faint, childish giggles echoed through the decaying hallways of the old toy shop, the sound both eerie and disorienting. My heart skipped a beat, the sound of those innocent giggles twisting into something far more sinister.

"This isn't good," Cassidy whispered, her voice trembling as she looked around, her eyes wide with fear. "Midas, something's wrong. We need to get out of here."

Sierra piped up, "She's right! We're not ready. We can't do this here!"

I nodded, the urgency of the situation hitting me like a punch to the gut. We had stirred up something dark, something that didn't want us there, and it was making its presence known.

The toy shop seemed to come alive around us, the very walls groaning under the weight of Thornton's malevolence.

The doors slammed shut on their own, the sound reverberating through the building like a gunshot. The windows rattled in their frames, the glass panes shuddering as if something was trying to break through.

An unseen force began to push against us, pressing down on our chests, making it hard to breathe.

Cassidy gasped, her hand flying to her throat as if she were being choked by invisible hands. "Midas," she tried to whisper as I grabbed her hand.

I could feel the pressure too, the overwhelming sense that something was trying to crush life out of us. My vision blurred as the air grew thinner, the darkness closing in around us, thick and suffocating.

Joshua and Sierra were choking and gagging as they hurried to the front door. I had no idea where Macie and Jericho were.

Then, out of the corner of my eye, I saw it—a shadowy figure materializing in the far corner of the room, barely visible in the dim light. My heart lurched in my chest as the figure took shape, slowly stepping into the light.

*Heinrich Thornton.*

He was tall, impossibly tall, his limbs unnaturally long, his figure stretched and distorted like something out of a nightmare. His face was a twisted mask of grotesque features, his eyes burning with an unnatural fire, his mouth stretched into a grotesque, twisted smile that sent a wave of terror crashing through me.

*He was the Tall Man!*

"Get out!" I yelled, my voice raw with fear as I reached for Cassidy's arm, pulling her toward the door. But the door wouldn't budge, held fast by the force of Thornton's spirit.

The walls shook violently, the very foundation of the building quaking under the weight of his rage.

The air was thick with malevolence, pressing down on us like a physical weight, and I could feel the darkness closing in, trying to snuff us out. My heart pounded in my chest, adrenaline surging through my veins as I shoved Cassidy toward the back door.

"Move, Cassidy! Now!" She stumbled, her breath coming in ragged gasps as she fought against the force that held us in place. I scooped her up in my arms.

Across the room, the strange manifestation of the spirit of Heinrich Thornton's twisted smile grew wider, his figure looming over us, his presence filling the room with a sense of dread so powerful it was almost tangible. Jericho and Macie were suddenly there beside me.

Together, we pushed harder, the door finally giving way under the pressure.

Cassidy and I tumbled out into the humidity and the natural air as we gasped for breath as the building shook violently behind us. The others were already outside, their faces pale and drawn, their eyes wide with terror. We barely made it out before the toy shop groaned and trembled, the windows shattering as Thornton's spirit lashed out in fury.

The sound of breaking glass filled the air, the building shaking as if it were about to collapse in on itself. We stumbled back, our hearts racing, as the full force of Thornton's rage tore through the shop.

For a moment, all I could do was stand there, panting, my chest heaving as I tried to catch my breath. The malevolent presence that had filled the toy shop was still in there, pressing down on us, watching us from the darkness.

But we had made it out. Barely.

I exchanged a glance with Cassidy, the fear still raw in her eyes, but there was something else there too—a resolve to see this through to the end. Thornton wasn't going to let the souls go without a fight, but we weren't going to back down.

Not now.

We had come too far to turn back. Thornton's spirit was strong, but we were stronger. We had to be.

And we weren't done yet.

# Chapter Ten–Midas

The weight of what lay ahead pressed down on us as we gathered in my hotel room. The air was thick with tension, a palpable sense of dread that hung over us like a storm cloud ready to burst.

The day's events had shaken us all to the core, but we knew we couldn't afford to let fear rule our actions now. The spirits of the trapped children depended on us, and we were their only hope of release.

Cassidy was the first to speak, her voice a whisper in the heavy silence. "I had another vision," she said, her eyes distant as if she were still caught in the throes of whatever she had seen. "There's a pit beneath the shop, a dark place…a place where the children's spirits are trapped. They were trying to claw their way out, but something was holding them back, something too strong for them to fight alone. I sketched it—it's not pretty."

I accepted the sketchbook and groaned at the sight. As a father, this sketch broke me in ways I hadn't expected.

The image sent a chill down my spine, the idea of those innocent child souls trapped in the dark, unable to break free. Seeing the pale, desperate faces of the children, their small hands bloodied and raw as they scratched at the walls of their prison, trying to escape the hell that Thornton had created for them broke my heart.

Jericho nodded, his expression grim. "We'll need more than just our usual protection for this. Thornton's spirit is strong, fueled by rage and sorrow that's festered for over a century. I've gathered some protective charms—symbols of purity and light—but we'll need to convince the children's spirits to break free from his control. I think we're going to have to distract Heinrich and while that's happening, the mediums can open the door for the dead."

I could see the resolve in his eyes, the fire that burned beneath his calm exterior.

Jericho had become our rock in spiritual and religious matters, the one who could keep his head when everything around us was falling apart.

"We'll only have one shot at this," I said, my voice steady despite the fear gnawing at my insides. "We need to be precise; we need to be prepared, and we need to be together on this. No mistakes. No hesitations. If we mess this up, there won't be a second chance. My question is where do we start? He's all over this town, or pieces of him are, guys."

Sierra, who had been pacing the room with nervous energy, stopped in her tracks. "We need to start at the playground," she said, her tone firm. "We cleanse it, sever Thornton's connection to the spirits there, and then move to the tree where he was hung. We've already blessed the Harris house, but Susan and Sabra need to be far away from here until this is over. It's not safe for them."

Macie added, "We may have to bless that house again. I bet you anything, he's going to want to go back there because Sabra is there. Or was there. He's willing to wait."

I nodded in agreement, the plan taking shape in my mind. "Y'all are right. We'll have to do this in stages, each step building on the last. The playground is where it all began, where Thornton's spirit first started its twisted game. We sever his hold there, then move to the tree—Thornton's point of death, the anchor that ties him to this world. We'll need every ounce of power we can muster to cleanse that spot."

Sierra pulled out her phone, already dialing Susan Harris's number. "I'll make the call to Susan," she said, her voice a mix of urgency and determination. "Susan needs to understand what's at stake. If she and Sabra stay, they'll be in danger, but if they leave now, they can come back to a home that's finally free of this nightmare."

The room fell into a tense silence as we listened to Sierra's side of the conversation.

Her voice was calm but firm as she explained the situation to Susan, laying out the necessity of their departure without sugarcoating the risks.

I could see the tension in her shoulders as she spoke, the weight of responsibility pressing down on her.

"Thank you, Susan," Sierra said finally, her voice softening. "We'll keep you updated. Just trust us. We'll take care of this. And leave the key under the mat in case we need to get back into the house. I'll call you when it is finished."

She ended the call and turned back to us, her eyes filled with the same resolve that burned in each of us. "They're leaving town tonight. We have a clear path to do what needs to be done."

I felt a surge of determination rise within me, a fierce need to see this through to the end. We had faced down spirits before, had walked through the valley of shadows more times than I could count, but this...this was different.

This was a battle not just for the children's spirits, but for the town of Huntsville itself, for the living who would be forever haunted by Thornton's evil if we failed.

"All right," I said, my voice cutting through the heavy silence. "We have our plan. We go to the playground, sever Thornton's connection there, and then move to the tree. We'll need to work fast, keep our focus sharp, and trust each other."

The others nodded, their eyes locked on mine, and I felt a surge of pride in my team. We had been through hell together, had faced down darkness and walked away stronger for it. This was just another test, another fight we had to win.

"We leave at dusk," I said, my voice firm. "Get your gear, say your prayers, and be ready. Tonight, we end this."

The drive to the playground was altogether too short. Were we truly ready?

The darkness crept in slowly, like a living thing, curling around the trees and playground equipment, casting long, sinister shadows that danced in the fading light. The air was thick with an almost palpable tension, the kind that made your skin prickle and your breath catch in your throat.

We all felt it—Thornton's presence, his malevolence seeping into every corner of this cursed playground.

We gathered at the center of the playground, the swings swaying gently in the wind, their rusty chains creaking like old bones. The ground beneath our feet felt wrong, as though it were alive, pulsating with a dark energy that resonated through the soles of my boots and up into my chest.

I could feel it in my bones—this was a place where the veil between the living and the dead was thin, where evil had taken root and festered for too long.

Jericho handed out the St. Michael's medallions, one to each of us, the cold metal heavy in my hand. These were more than just symbols; they were our lifeline, our protection against the darkness that threatened to swallow us whole.

"We'll bury these at the four corners," I said, my voice low but steady, though my heart was hammering in my chest. "We'll scatter the blessed salt around the perimeter to seal it. Sierra? Either you or Cassidy, you take the lead with the ritual. Call the children forward, let them know we're here to help. That needs to happen before the circle is completed or they'll be trapped inadvertently."

"I'd like to try," Cassidy nodded, her face set with determination, though I could see the fear lurking in her eyes. We all felt it—the weight of what we were about to do, the risk we were taking. But there was no turning back now. "Sierra, stay close though," she smiled at her. I wanted to speak up and say no but that would hardly be fair. I couldn't hide her from the paranormal just because she was my wife.

The air crackled with energy as we began to move, each of us taking a corner of the playground, burying the medallions deep in the earth.

The ground resisted, as though it didn't want to let go of its dark secrets, but we pressed on, our hands working quickly in the dying light.

As we scattered the blessed salt, a sudden chill swept through the playground, the temperature plummeting in an instant. I could see my breath misting in the air, could feel the icy fingers of fear wrapping around my heart.

The wind picked up, swirling the leaves around our feet, carrying with it the faint, mournful cries of children long dead.

That's when I saw her—a woman, dressed in black, her figure tall and imposing as she stepped out from the shadows. Her eyes were dark, cold, and full of malice as she approached us, her lips curled into a sneer.

She was the woman from the car, the one that watched us working in the playground before that storm erupted. Everything about her screamed, "EVIL!"

"What do you think you're doing here?" she demanded, her voice sharp, cutting through the night like a blade. "You have no authority here."

Sierra stepped forward, her stance firm, her voice unwavering. "You know what we're doing," she said, her eyes locked onto the woman's. "And you can't stop us."

The woman's lips curled into a twisted smile, her eyes narrowing to slits. "Can't I?" she hissed, her tone dripping with venom. "He's mine to command, and I'm not ready to let him go. Turn around and go back to where you came from, or you'll regret it, pretty lady. Go now or face the consequences."

A surge of anger rose within me, but I held it in check, my mind racing to understand who this woman was, what her connection to Thornton might be. Her presence here wasn't a coincidence—she was tied to this, to him, and she wasn't going to let us end it without a fight. With a wicked grin she turned and walked back toward her car.

"My turn," Cassidy whispered, her voice barely audible over the wind that had begun to howl through the trees.

She stepped forward, her voice strong as she began the ritual, her words clear and commanding. "Spirits of the lost, hear us. We are here to free you, to break the chains that bind you. Come forward, let us help you find peace."

The air around us seemed to vibrate with a dark power, the ground beneath our feet humming with a malevolent energy that grew stronger with each passing second.

Shadows flitted at the edge of my vision, darting in and out of the darkness, their forms indistinct but filled with a sense of impending doom.

The woman's face twisted with fury as Cassidy's words took hold, as the ritual began to take effect. "Stop it!" she screamed, her voice shrill, grating against my ears like nails on a chalkboard. But Cassidy didn't falter, her voice rising above the howling wind, above the dark energy that swirled around us.

"Spirits of the lost, hear me. We are here to free you, to break the chains that bind you. Come forward, children, let us help you find peace."

Jericho stepped forward, his voice low and steady as he began to whisper a prayer, his words a shield against the darkness that threatened to consume us. He was praying it what he called an "angelic language" and it was proving to have an effect on the unwanted woman.

*What was she doing harnessing an evil ghost like Heinrich Thornton? Oh yeah. Witch. Not a good one either.*

Immediately stood closer to Cassidy. The woman's eyes flashed with rage, and for a moment, I thought she might strike out at us, might try to stop the ritual with force. But then, something changed.

Jericho's voice got louder, the wind began to move, not from the trees down but in the grass and shrubs.

The dark worker's eyes widened in fear, her confidence faltering as Jericho's words took hold, as the power of the prayer pushed back against the malevolence that surrounded us.

With a snarl of frustration, and a string of swear words, she turned on her heel and ran, her footsteps echoing in the night as she fled the playground.

I heard the slam of a car door, the roar of an engine, and then she was gone, leaving us alone in the oppressive darkness.

"Hurry, Jericho!" I shouted, my voice filled with urgency. "She'll be back, and she won't be alone. We need to finish this, now! Cassidy, keep going!"

The wind howled around us, the swings creaking and groaning as they swayed in the storm's fury.

I could feel Thornton's anger, his desperate attempts to hold on to the spirits, to keep them trapped in his twisted world. The ground shook beneath our feet, the very earth protesting our presence, but we pressed on, our resolve unshaken.

Cassidy's voice grew louder, her words ringing out like a beacon in the darkness. "Spirits of the lost, break free! Come forward and find peace, children! We are here to help you, to end your suffering!"

The ground beneath us trembled, and for a moment, I thought it might open and swallow us whole. The darkness pressed in from all sides, the air thick with Thornton's rage, with the weight of the evil that had taken root in this place.

But then, slowly, the tide began to turn.

The darkness that had surrounded us began to recede, the oppressive energy lifting as the spirits of the children began to come forward, their forms faint but unmistakable. I could see them, their faces pale and sad, their eyes wide with fear and confusion.

"We're here to help you," I said, adding my voice to Cassidy's and Jericho's. "You don't have to be afraid anymore. Thornton—the Tall Man can't hurt you. Not anymore."

The spirits hesitated, their small forms flickering in and out of sight, as though they were struggling to break free from the chains that bound them. I could feel Thornton's presence, his anger growing with each passing second, but we held our ground, our resolve unshaken.

"Come forward," Cassidy urged, her voice filled with compassion. "It's time to be free."

"We need to move," I said, my voice urgent. "We need to finish this. Before it's too late."

The playground, once eerily still, now came alive with a fury that shook the very ground beneath us. Thornton's spirit had been pushed to the edge, and he wasn't about to let go without a fight.

As Cassidy continued calling on the spirits of the children to come forward, the air around us grew colder, the temperature plummeting to an unnatural chill that made my breath come out in visible puffs.

Then, without warning, a blast of icy wind slammed into Cassidy, nearly knocking her off her feet. She stumbled, her voice faltering for a moment, but she quickly regained her balance, her resolve unbroken.

The swings that had once swayed gently now moved violently, the rusty chains clanging like an ominous warning. The slide shuddered as if something massive was trying to rip it from the ground.

A low, guttural growl echoed through the playground, deep and menacing, the sound vibrating through my bones.

It grew louder, more intense, and I realized with a sinking heart that Thornton was far from done. He was gathering his strength, his rage building to a terrifying crescendo. The darkness around us thickened, pressing in, suffocating. Then he appeared.

Thornton's spirit, towering and twisted, materialized before us, his form impossibly tall, his presence oppressive and malevolent. His eyes, black as the void, locked onto Cassidy, and I could see the raw hatred burning within them.

I opened my mouth to scream, to warn her, but no sound came out.

My throat constricted, my muscles locked in place—I was paralyzed, held in place by Thornton's will. I couldn't move either and my wife, well, she was now in the monster's crosshairs.

Cassidy stood frozen, her eyes wide with terror as the Tall Man loomed over her, his long, skeletal fingers reaching out. She stepped back blindly as he moved with a terrifying grace, each step deliberate, as if savoring the fear that radiated from my poor wife.

I could see the panic in her eyes, the realization that she couldn't escape, that none of us could. That I couldn't reach her.

I tried to yell for help, but nobody could move. My team was powerless to help Cassidy or me. This monster commanded a silent presence.

I could feel the tears flow as Thornton's hand wrapped around Cassidy's throat, lifting her off the ground with ease. She gasped, her hands clawing at the evil force that choked her, but there was no escape. His grip tightened, and I could see the life draining from her, her eyes wide with terror.

Somehow, Jericho's voice rose above the chaos, his prayers growing louder, more fervent, as he tried to break Thornton's hold. But Thornton was strong, fueled by a rage that had festered for over a century and likely fueled by the human agents, like the dark witch, that had summoned him for their own nefarious reasons.

He had no intention of letting Cassidy go.

With his other hand, the Tall Man reached for Cassidy's belly, his fingers unnaturally long, like talons ready to rip her apart. But then, he paused, his head tilting to the side as if listening to something only he could hear. A twisted smile spread across his face, his black eyes narrowing with malevolent delight.

"Ah," he purred, his voice a deep, unnatural rumble. "I smell it. I smell the baby. Let me have it. Give it to me. *Gib es mir*!" I didn't speak German but I knew he didn't have any good intentions for us.

Cassidy's screams were muffled by Thornton's grip. She kicked and thrashed, but it was no use. He held her easily, like a doll, his strength inhuman.

"Midas!" The rest of us were powerless, frozen in place by the malevolent force that radiated from Thornton.

Tears flowed down my face as I watched my wife struggle against the evil being. I finally found my voice.

"No! Leave her alone! Come at me, you bastard!"

Just when it seemed that all hope was lost, Joshua managed to break free from the paralyzing grip that held us. With a burst of strength, he pushed me, breaking the hold that Thornton had over me.

The moment I could move, I was running, adrenaline surging through me as I raced toward Cassidy and the tall spindly creature that threatened.

Thornton's grip on her loosened slightly, and with a primal growl of frustration, he dropped her to the ground. But he wasn't done. Resting on his haunches, his limbs twisted and elongated, he sat on all fours but I had no doubt he would move with a speed and agility that was nothing short of terrifying.

Still, we had to make a break for it.

"Run, honey! Everyone!" I shouted, grabbing Cassidy's hand and pulling her to her feet. We bolted out of the playground, the sound of Thornton's growls echoing in our ears, his twisted form chasing us with relentless determination.

"Stay in the circle!" Jericho's voice called after us, but there was no turning us back. All I could think about was protecting my wife.

The circle might have protected us, but Thornton was stronger than we had anticipated, and the fear driving us was too overwhelming to ignore.

The ground beneath our feet trembled as we ran, the earth itself seeming to rebel against us.

Spectral hands reached out from the shadows, grasping at our legs, trying to pull us back into the darkness. The air was thick with the stench of decay, the oppressive weight of Thornton's malevolence pressing down on us from all sides.

Cassidy's breath came in ragged gasps as we sprinted through the night, her hand gripping mine like a lifeline. Thornton's laughter, deep and mocking, followed us, growing louder, closer, as if he was toying with us, enjoying the chase.

We were nearing the edge of the playground when the ground beneath us gave a violent lurch. I stumbled, nearly losing my footing, but Cassidy's grip on my hand kept me upright. The swings were now whipping back and forth with a force that could snap bones, the slide shuddering as if ready to collapse.

"Keep going!" I shouted, my voice hoarse with fear and exhaustion. "We have to get you out of here!"

The air around us crackled with energy, the darkness pressing in from all sides, and I could feel Thornton's presence growing stronger, more malevolent.

The ritual had weakened him, but it hadn't been enough. He was still here, still hunting us, still determined to claim Cassidy and our unborn child.

*Another child? Why didn't she tell me?*

With a final, desperate burst of energy, we broke free of the playground, the oppressive weightlifting slightly as we crossed the boundary. But I knew we weren't safe. Thornton was still out there, still lurking in the shadows, waiting for his moment to strike.

Jericho's voice echoed in the distance, his prayers growing louder, more frantic, as he and the others tried to hold the circle, to keep Thornton contained. But I knew it was only a matter of time before he broke through.

"We can't stop, baby," I panted, pulling Cassidy along as we raced toward the relative safety of the streetlights. "We have to keep moving!"

"Okay!" She whispered savagely as we traveled through a minefield of gravestones.

Thornton's growls echoed behind us, growing fainter as we put distance between us and the playground. But I knew this wasn't over. He wasn't done with us—not by a long shot.

As we reached the edge of the park, the streetlights casting long shadows on the pavement, I dared to look back. The playground was shrouded in darkness, the swings still moving, the slide still trembling. And in the center of it all, I saw him—Thornton, standing tall and menacing, his eyes glowing with an unnatural light.

He wasn't just a ghost. He was something much worse.

Something that wouldn't rest until he had claimed what he believed was his.

"Get to the van!" I shouted; my voice filled with a fear I hadn't felt in years. "We must regroup. This isn't over."

We reached the van and scrambled inside, slamming the doors behind us, the silence that followed almost deafening. My heart was pounding in my chest, my breath coming in short, sharp gasps as I tried to process what had just happened.

Thornton was stronger than we had anticipated, more dangerous.

And I knew, deep down, that this was only the beginning.

# Chapter Eleven–Sierra

The playground was a battlefield, the air thick with tension and fear, but I wasn't about to run. I couldn't.

The Tall Man's presence loomed, heavy and suffocating, pressing down on us like a dark cloud that threatened to swallow everything. But even as the others hesitated, their instincts screaming at them to flee, something deep within me held firm.

Not that I blamed Midas. *Who knew Cassidy was pregnant? That explains why I've been feeling so dang sick.* But I wasn't going to let Thornton win. Not after everything we had been through.

The darkness around us was alive, shifting and pulsing with an energy that I could feel in my bones. It wasn't just the night—it was Thornton, his rage, his hatred, his twisted need to control, to dominate.

The air crackled with his malevolence, and I knew he was close, watching, waiting for the right moment to strike. I sensed his attention shift. He'd given up his attack on Cassidy and Midas. Thornton was coming back to keep his treasures enslaved.

But I also knew something else.

The children—their spirits—were here too. I could feel them, sense their presence like a soft whisper at the edge of my mind. They'd been drawn to Cassidy's sweet spirit and Jericho's angelic language had pushed back the darkness long enough for the children to see the light.

Their little souls were trapped, bound to this place by Thornton's twisted will, but they weren't gone. Not yet. And if they were still here, there was hope. I suspected there were bodies under the old toy store, but this would do.

The children were coming, rising and I could feel them.

I closed my eyes for a moment, blocking out the noise, the fear, the rising panic in my chest. I had to focus, had to reach out to them, to make them see that they weren't alone, that we were here to help.

They had been lost for so long, forgotten, but not anymore.

We were going to free them, no matter what it took.

When I opened my eyes again, the playground had changed. The shadows had deepened, lengthened, stretching out like dark tendrils that seemed to reach for us, but I wasn't afraid. I could see them now—the children.

They were everywhere, crawling up from the ground, their small hands clawing at the earth as they pulled themselves free. The sight of them took my breath away. Others emerged from the bushes, their wide, haunted eyes glowing with a pale, ghostly light.

My heart ached at the sight of them, so small, so lost, their spirits fragile and flickering like candle flames in the wind. But they were here, and that meant there was still a chance.

A chance to save them, to break the chains that Thornton had wrapped around their souls.

I could feel his presence emerging, the air around us thickening with his anger, his determination to keep what he believed was his. But I wasn't going to let him. Not this time. Not ever.

I took a deep breath, my hands clenched into fists at my sides as I prepared for what was to come.

This was it. The final battle. And I wasn't backing down.

"Jericho! Macie! I need your help!" I shouted to the others. Joshua was already next to me. He kept the camera hoisted on his shoulder somehow or another.

The children's spirits were all around us now, their ghostly forms flickering in and out of existence, like faint echoes of a time long past. Their eyes, so full of fear and confusion, locked onto mine, and I could feel their longing, their desperate need for peace, for release from the nightmare that had trapped them here for so long

I took a step forward, my heart pounding in my chest as I reached out with my mind, with my soul, trying to connect with them, to make them see that they weren't alone, that they could fight back.

I could feel Thornton's presence pressing down on us, a heavy, suffocating force that seemed to sap the strength from my limbs, but I pushed it aside, focusing on the children, on their spirits, on the light that still flickered within them.

I got the distinct impression that he was weak, weaker than he'd been in a long time.

"You don't have to be afraid, children," I whispered, my voice trembling with emotion as I spoke to them, as I tried to reach through the darkness, through the fear, to the part of them that still remembered what it was like to be free.

Jericho joined me and spoke softly. "You're not alone. We're here to help you, to set you free. But we can't do it without you. We need your help. Please, you must fight back. You have to stand up to him."

For a moment, there was nothing but silence, the oppressive weight of Thornton's presence pressing down on us, threatening to crush the life out of me. But then, slowly, I began to feel a shift—a subtle change in the energy around us, as if the children were beginning to understand, to believe.

Their fear was still there, but it was joined by something else—determination, resolve, a glimmer of hope that hadn't been there before.

"Yes," I murmured, my voice barely audible over the sound of the wind rustling through the trees. "You can do this. You can fight back. Don't let him control you anymore. You're stronger than he is. You're stronger together."

"She's right," Macie said with a smile on her face. I could see the fear in her eyes, but the children needed to see us confident and ready to help them.

I could feel the energy building, the light within the children's spirits growing brighter, and stronger, as they began to stand, to rise against the darkness that had held them captive for so long.

Thornton's presence was still there, threatening us, but it was weakening, the chains that bound the children beginning to crack, to break under the weight of their collective will.

But it wasn't enough. Not yet. We needed more, needed to push harder, to break through the last of Thornton's defenses. And that's when it hit me—we needed to encircle him, to trap him, just as he had trapped the children.

Jericho turned to me and spoke quickly, "We need to turn his own tactics against him, to use the power of the children's spirits to form a barrier, a circle of light that would hold him, contain him, and ultimately banish him for good."

"Form a circle," I called out, my voice rising above the wind, above the darkness that surrounded us. "We need to surround him, to break his hold. We can do this, but we must work together." I clutched Jericho's and Joshua's hands. Macie completed the circle.

The children hesitated for a moment, their eyes wide with fear, but then, one by one, they began to move, their small hands reaching out to one another, forming a circle around the playground. Their spirits were flickering, and fragile, but their determination was growing, their will to fight back against Thornton's darkness becoming stronger with each passing second.

I could feel the energy building, the light within them growing brighter, and stronger, as they joined forces, their spirits united against the malevolent presence that had held them captive for so long.

And then, in the center of the circle, I saw him—Thornton, the Tall Man, his twisted form looming above us, his eyes burning with rage. He towered over the children, his presence a black void that threatened to swallow them whole.

But they didn't back down. They stood their ground, their circle unbroken around us, their combined will pushing back against Thornton's malevolence, against the darkness that had held them captive for so long.

Joshua's face was set with determination. His presence gave me strength, grounding me in the moment, even as the world seemed to tilt and shift around us. I was grateful for his calming presence. I loved him so much.

The playground had become a battlefield, and I could feel the weight of every lost spirit pressing down on us, urging us forward, but I wasn't alone. None of us were. Thank God none of the public could witness this paranormal showdown. There hadn't been a soul on the street the whole time we'd been here. It was almost as if we were hidden in plain sight by the paranormal.

As I focused, my hands outstretched, I felt the energy around us begin to hum, to vibrate with a strange, almost musical resonance.

The children's spirits were moving, responding to my call, to the pull of the energy that connected us all. I could feel their fear, their confusion, but I could also sense their longing, their desperate need for peace, for release. They had been trapped in this place for so long, held captive by Thornton's twisted will, but now, they were fighting back.

"Come on, children," I whispered, my voice barely audible over the howling wind, and the rustle of the trees. "You can do this. You're stronger than he is. You've always been stronger."

Joshua clutched my hand tighter and I felt a surge of warmth, of strength, as if the connection between us had somehow amplified the energy, the light that was building within the circle.

The children were moving now, their small hands clasped together, their faces set with determination. They were ready to fight, to stand up to the darkness that had held them captive for so long.

But it wasn't just about them.

I could feel the energy building, growing stronger with each passing second, as the children's spirits began to encircle the Tall Man, their light flickering, pulsing, as they pushed back against his darkness.

"Don't let him win," I whispered, my voice trembling with emotion. "You're not alone. We're all in this together."

The air around us seemed to crackle with energy, with the combined will of the living and the dead, as we stood together against Thornton's malevolence. I could feel the pressure building, the weight of the moment pressing down on us, but I wasn't afraid.

Not anymore. This was it—the final stand, the last push against the darkness that had haunted this place for so long.

And then, in that moment, I knew—we were going to win.

We were going to free these children, to break the chains that bound them, to banish Thornton once and for all. We were stronger than he was, stronger together, and there was no way he could stand against the combined force of our will, our determination.

The light within the circle grew brighter, and stronger, as the children's spirits moved closer, their hands clasped together, their eyes locked on Thornton's twisted form.

I could see the fear in his eyes, the realization that he was losing, that his time was running out. But I didn't let up. I pushed harder, reaching out with my mind, with my soul, urging the children forward, urging them to fight, to break free.

And then, with a surge of energy, of power, the circle closed in around Thornton, the light of the children's spirits burning bright, blinding, as it engulfed him, tearing through his darkness, shattering the chains that bound them.

I could feel the connection deepening, strengthening, as Jericho joined me, his voice steady and calm as he whispered words of encouragement, of power.

Together, we were creating a bridge, a conduit between the living and the dead, a pathway through which the children's voices could be heard, and their spirits could be freed.

The air around us seemed to shimmer with energy, with the combined force of our will, our determination.

Jericho's voice was a steady anchor, grounding me even as the world seemed to tilt and shift around us. I could feel the pressure building, the weight of the moment pressing down on us, but I wasn't afraid.

"Listen to them," Jericho murmured, his voice soft but powerful, his words carrying through the night like a beacon of light. "They're trying to reach you, trying to help you. You just have to listen."

The children's spirits were moving now, their light flickering, pulsing, as they pushed back against Thornton's darkness.

I could feel their fear, their confusion, but I could also sense their strength, their determination. They were ready to fight, to stand up to the darkness that had held them captive for so long.

And then, I felt it—a surge of energy, of power, as the children's spirits began to move, their light growing brighter, stronger, as they encircled the Tall Man, their hands clasped together, their eyes locked on his twisted form. I could see the fear in his eyes, the realization that he was losing, that his time was running out.

But I didn't let up. I pushed harder, reaching out with my mind, with my soul, urging the children forward, urging them to fight, to break free. The air around us seemed to hum with energy, with the combined force of our will, our determination. We were stronger than he was, stronger together, and there was no way he could stand against the combined force of our will, our determination.

Jericho's voice continued to be a steady anchor, grounding us all even as the world seemed to swirl around us.

I could feel the pressure building, the weight of the moment pressing down on us, but I wasn't afraid. Not anymore. This was it—the final stand, the last push against the darkness that had haunted this place for so long.

"Stay with me," I whispered, my voice trembling with emotion. "We're almost there. Don't let go. Don't let him win."

I could see the fear in the evil entity's eyes, the realization that he was losing, that his time was running out. We didn't let up. I pushed harder, reaching out with my mind, with my soul, urging the children forward, urging them to fight, to break free.

And then, with a surge of energy, of power, the circle closed in around Thornton, the light of the children's spirits burning bright, blinding, as it engulfed him, tearing through his darkness, shattering the chains that bound them.

The air around us shimmered, pulsed with energy, as I called out to the children's families, their spirits hovering at the edge of my awareness, waiting, watching.

I could feel them, sense their presence like a whisper in the wind, a distant memory that had been buried deep within the earth for far too long. They were here, just beyond the veil, waiting for the moment when they could step forward, when they could join the battle that was raging all around us.

I closed my eyes, focusing on the connection, on the bond that linked us all together, on the thread of energy that wove through the fabric of the night, binding us to the children, to their families, to the spirits that had been lost for so long.

I could feel their pain, their sorrow, their longing for peace, for release from the darkness that had held them captive for so many years.

I knew they were ready to stand up to the Tall Man, to push back against the darkness that had consumed them.

"Come forward, little ones," I whispered, my voice trembling with emotion as I reached out with my mind, with my soul, urging them to step forward, to join the circle, to lend their strength to the battle that was unfolding all around us. "You're not alone. We're here to help you, to set you free. But we can't do it without you. We need your help. Please, come forward."

The air around us seemed to crackle with energy, with the combined force of our will, our determination. The ground beneath my feet trembled, the darkness pressing in from all sides, but I didn't waver.

I held my ground, focusing on the connection, on the bond that linked us all together, on the light that was growing stronger with each passing second.

And then, slowly, I felt them move—the spirits of the children's families, their light flickering, pulsing, as they stepped forward, as they joined the circle that had formed around the playground.

The Tall Man, Thornton, his presence growing stronger, more oppressive, as he fought to hold on to the control he had maintained for so long. But we were stronger.

Together, we were stronger. The light within the circle grew brighter, stronger, as the spirits of the children's families joined forces with the children, their hands clasped together, their eyes locked on Thornton's twisted form.

The ground beneath us trembled, shook with a force that seemed to come from deep within the earth itself, as Thornton's spirit fought back, lashing out with a fury that was palpable, tangible, a wave of darkness that threatened to swallow us whole.

The air around us crackled with energy, with the force of his rage, his determination to hold on to the control he had maintained for so long.

But we didn't waver. We didn't back down.

The circle held, the light within it growing brighter, stronger, as the spirits of the children, and their families, pushed back against Thornton's darkness, against the malevolent force that had held them captive for so many years.

Thornton's form wavered, flickered at the edges as the light of the children's spirits, their families' spirits, burned brighter, tearing through the darkness that had held them captive.

*"No! You cannot have them! They are mine! All mine!"* He fought back, swinging his wildly long arms and legs, lashing out with a force that sent shockwaves through the ground, through the air, but it wasn't enough.

The light within the circle grew brighter as we pushed back, as we fought to break the chains that had bound these spirits for so long.

The ground beneath us shook with a force that nearly knocked me off my feet, but I held on, focusing on the connection, on the bond that linked us all together, on the light that was growing brighter with each passing second.

The ground beneath Thornton shook, threatening to open beneath him. Yes, I could see it!

A pit of darkness from which spectral hands reached out, grasping at his form, pulling him down into the earth. His roar of rage and defiance echoed through the night, but it was quickly swallowed by the light, by the combined force of the spirits that had revolted against him.

The hands of the dead, the children he had tormented, the families he had terrorized, pulled him down, down into the earth, into the darkness from which he would never return.

And then, just like that, with a horrible roar, it was over and all then went silent.

The ground closed up, the pit of darkness sealed, and the light of the children's spirits, their families' spirits, faded into the night, their forms dissolving into the ether as they finally found the peace they had been denied for so long.

The playground fell silent, the oppressive energy lifting, the darkness that had haunted this place for so long finally banished.

I stood there, my breath coming in ragged gasps, my heart pounding in my chest, as the reality of what we had just done settled over me.

We had won. We had freed the children, banished Thornton, and broken the chains that had bound these spirits for so long. The playground was quiet now, peaceful, the oppressive energy lifted, the darkness banished. But the memory of what we had faced, of the battle we had fought, would stay with me forever.

This was not just another case.

This was a battle between light and darkness, between good and evil, and we had won.

We had freed the children, banished Thornton, and brought peace to a place that had known only sorrow and pain for so long.

The night was quiet now, the playground went still, as the light of the spirits faded into the ether, leaving behind only the memory of their presence, their struggle, their victory.

We had done it. We had won.

But the cost had been high, and the memory of what we had faced, of what we had fought, would stay with us forever.

# Chapter Twelve–Midas

The sound of my own breathing filled the small space of the SUV, harsh and ragged. My chest felt tight, constricted with the lingering terror of what had just happened. I pushed away the chest pain, pretending that it hadn't been nagging me for weeks. I told myself it was merely anxiety, but I couldn't be sure.

Cassidy was holding me, her arms wrapped around me like she was the only thing anchoring me to this world. I couldn't stop shaking, couldn't stop the tears that kept streaming down my face, hot and uncontrollable.

I almost lost her. I almost lost her and I had been unable to help her. The helpless feeling was my worst nightmare.

"I almost lost you," I whispered, my voice breaking under the weight of the words. "Cassidy, I almost lost you. Enough of all this. Enough. I can't lose you, Cassidy."

She pulled back slightly, just enough to look me in the eyes, her gaze steady and filled with a strength I didn't feel.

"Hey! Look at me! You won't lose me, Midas," she said softly, her voice full of conviction. "You're stuck with me for a lifetime, longer if God allows."

I closed my eyes, leaning into her touch, letting the sound of her voice wash over me like balm to my shattered nerves. But the fear was still there, clawing at the edges of my mind, reminding me of just how close I'd come to losing her tonight.

The silence between us stretched on, heavy and thick with the weight of unspoken words. Finally, I managed to find my voice again, though it trembled as I spoke.

"Is it true? What was that about...Thornton? What he said..."

Cassidy's eyes flickered with something I couldn't quite place—fear, maybe, or uncertainty. But she didn't hesitate. She took a deep breath and nodded.

"Yes, it's true," she admitted, her voice barely above a whisper. "I'm pregnant. I was waiting for the right moment to tell you. You haven't seemed...open to talking about things lately." Her words hit me like a punch to the gut, knocking the breath right out of me.

Pregnant. Cassidy was pregnant again.

My mind reeled, struggling to process the reality of what she'd just said. She looked away, her gaze falling to her hands, which were trembling slightly. "I didn't want to add more pressure to your life," she admitted, her voice barely audible. "Are we ready for another baby? Dom is barely walking."

"Yes, we're ready. We can do anything together. Hey, tell me you're excited about this."

The guilt hit me like a wave, crashing over me and leaving me gasping for air. I had been distant, lost in my own head, too wrapped up in the darkness of our cases to notice what was happening right in front of me. And now...now Cassidy was pregnant, and I hadn't even been there for her.

I reached out, taking her hands in mine, holding them tight as if I could somehow make up for all the time I'd wasted, all the moments I hadn't been there.

"Of course I am excited. The world needs all the Demopolis's it can hold. I'm sorry," I whispered, my voice thick with emotion. "Cassidy, I'm so sorry. I should have been there for you."

She looked up at me then, her eyes filled with tears, but there was a small, sad smile on her lips. "We've both been through a lot," she said softly. "But we'll get through this too, Midas. We always do."

I pulled her into my arms, holding her as tight as I could, afraid to let go, afraid that if I did, I'd lose her forever. The fear was still there, gnawing at the edges of my mind, but there was something else now too—hope.

Hope that maybe, just maybe, we could find our way back to each other, that we could make it through this, together. But the world outside was still waiting for us, the darkness still lurking just beyond the edges of the SUV.

As much as I wanted to stay here, in this moment, holding Cassidy and forgetting about everything else, I knew we couldn't.

"We need to go back," I said quietly, my voice filled with a determination that surprised even me. "The team...they need us. We can't leave them to face this alone."

Cassidy nodded, pulling back slightly, though she kept her hands clasped tightly in mine. "You're right," she said, her voice steady. "We need to help them."

The windows of the SUV were fogged up, the condensation thick and obscuring our view of the world outside. I wiped a hand across the glass, trying to clear a small section so we could see, but it was no use.

All I could see was a blur of shapes, indistinct and unrecognizable.

And then, all of a sudden, the doors of the SUV burst open, and the team poured inside, their faces pale and drawn, their breaths coming in sharp, ragged gasps. They were soaked through, shivering with cold and fear, but they were alive.

And that was all that mattered.

"We got him! We got the bastard!" Macie announced as she climbed in, soaked to the bone. It was pouring rain now. "That was close, y'all. Too close!"

The SUV felt cramped with all of us squeezed inside, our clothes soaked and sticking to our skin, the heat from our bodies steaming up the windows even more.

The rain outside was relentless, hammering against the roof and making it nearly impossible to hear anything except the pounding of our own hearts.

I looked around at my team—my family—and saw the same expression on every face: relief, yes, but also exhaustion, fear, and the weight of what we had just survived.

Macie, still catching her breath, wiped a hand across her face, pushing wet hair out of her eyes. "I swear, I thought he had us for a second there," she said, her voice still shaking slightly. "But we held on. We didn't let him win."

Cassidy reached out, placing a hand on Macie's arm, a silent gesture of comfort. "We didn't let him win," Cassidy repeated, her voice stronger now, more certain. "But we came damn close."

Jericho, sitting in the front seat, turned around to face us. "That was more than I expected. We knew Thornton was powerful, but that…that was something else. He wasn't just angry. He was desperate. We're lucky we made it out."

"Lucky?" I scoffed, though there was no humor in it. "Luck had nothing to do with it. That was all of you—your strength, your courage. You faced him down, and we survived. I've never been prouder of all of you."

Joshua, still visibly shaken, looked at me, his eyes wide with a mix of fear and determination. "What's our next move, Midas?"

I nodded, my mind racing through the possibilities. The pain in my chest intensified and I rubbed at my sternum as I considered his question. We had done something major tonight, but there was still loose ends to be tidy up. I couldn't wait to tell Susan and Sabra that they were safe.

"We need to regroup, get back to the hotel, and figure out where we go from here. We need to make sure Thornton cannot find a way back."

Cassidy squeezed my hand, her touch grounding me amid the chaos. "We'll take it one step at a time," she said softly. "But we'll get through this. Together."

I looked at her, my heart swelling with love and worry. "Cassidy, are you sure you're up for this? The baby…"

She smiled, though I could see the weariness in her eyes. "I'm fine, Midas. We're fine. But you're right—we need to be smart about this. We'll rest, get our heads straight, and then we'll finish this. All of us."

Macie nodded in agreement. "We've come too far to back down now. Thornton thought he could scare us off, but he was wrong."

Jericho leaned back in his seat, a thoughtful look on his face. "Let's not get cocky. We need to be prepared for whatever comes next. This fight...it's not just about Thornton. It's about all the spirits he's trapped, all the darkness he's brought to this place. We need to be ready to face it, no matter what. We need to make sure all the children are set free."

I took a deep breath, feeling the weight of the responsibility settling on my shoulders. But I wasn't alone. I had my team, and my family, with me, and together, we would see this through to the end.

As we started the SUV and began the drive back to the hotel, I couldn't help but feel a sense of finality mixed with anticipation.

The battle wasn't over, but we had won a crucial fight tonight.

And with my team by my side, I knew we could win the war.

# Chapter Thirteen–Cassidy

The room was steeped in darkness, the kind that made everything feel distant and unreal. I blinked, disoriented, as I woke from a dreamless sleep, a strange compulsion tugging at me.

My eyes adjusted slowly to the dim light filtering through the curtains, and I realized with a start that I was wide awake.

I could feel it, an urge gnawing at me from the inside, pulling me out of bed.

It wasn't fear, not exactly, but something close to it—a sense of urgency that I couldn't ignore. Without even thinking, I reached for my sketch pad and pencils, my fingers brushing over the familiar textures as I pulled them into my lap.

I didn't know what I was about to draw, but the compulsion was too strong to resist.

I needed to put pencil to paper, to let whatever was stirring inside me spill out. It was as if something or someone was guiding my hand, and I had no choice but to follow.

I slipped quietly out of bed, careful not to wake Midas, who was still sound asleep beside me. My bare feet touched the cool floor, sending a shiver up my spine as I tiptoed to the bathroom.

Closing the door behind me, I clicked on the bathroom light, the sudden brightness making me squint. The small space felt even more confined under the harsh glow, but it was exactly what I needed—a quiet place to work through this feeling that had taken hold of me.

I settled onto the cold tile floor, my back against the tub, and flipped open the sketch pad. The pencil felt solid in my hand, comforting in its familiarity. I stared at the blank page, my heart pounding in my chest, waiting for the inspiration to come. I had no idea what I was about to create, but deep down, I knew it was important—something I couldn't ignore.

With a deep breath, I pressed the pencil to the paper and began to draw.

The lines flowed effortlessly from my pencil, each stroke feeling more like instinct than thought.

My hand moved on its own, guided by an unseen force, as the image began to take shape on the page. I didn't question it; didn't stop to think about what I was drawing or why—I simply let it happen.

As the minutes ticked by, the picture became clearer and more defined. It started with the outline of a small face, delicate and soft, with eyes that seemed to stare straight into my soul. I worked slowly, carefully, adding details—wisps of hair framing her face, a small nose, and a gentle curve of lips that held a hint of a smile.

It wasn't until I reached the eyes that a sense of recognition began to creep in.

They were familiar, these eyes—wide and expressive, filled with warmth and curiosity. I paused, my pencil hovering over the page, my heart suddenly racing as I realized where I'd seen those eyes before.

They were Midas's eyes.

A sharp gasp escaped my lips, and I blinked, my mind reeling as I looked at the image on the page. The small face staring back at me was that of a child—a little girl with Midas's eyes and his dark, unruly hair. But there was something else, something in the shape of her face, the curve of her chin, that reminded me of someone else—someone I hadn't thought about in a long time.

Kylie. My sister, gone too soon. The resemblance between the two was uncanny despite Midas's darker skin tone and hair.

My breath caught in my throat, and I felt tears prickling at the corners of my eyes. This was my daughter, not my little sister.

The realization hit me like a tidal wave, overwhelming and undeniable. I was looking at the face of the child growing inside me, the daughter I hadn't even fully accepted I was carrying.

My hands trembled, the pencil slipping from my grasp as I stared at the sketch, my heart pounding in my chest. The emotions surged, a mix of joy, fear, and something deeper—something almost primal.

I was terrified, and yet...I couldn't look away.

The bathroom door creaked open behind me, and I jumped, startled out of my thoughts.

I turned to see Midas standing in the doorway, his face shadowed in concern. He looked tired, his hair tousled from sleep, but his eyes were alert, focused on me.

"Cassidy?" he murmured, his voice low and filled with worry. "What are you doing in here? You okay? Are you sick?"

I nodded, unable to find my voice at first. My emotions were still raw, my mind swirling with the realization of what I had just drawn. He sat down on the floor beside me.

I leaned my head on his shoulder, seeking comfort in his warmth, his steady presence.

He wrapped an arm around me as if to shield me from whatever had disturbed my peace. I closed my eyes for a moment, savoring the feel of him next to me, grounding me in the here and now.

"Would you like to meet someone?" I whispered, my voice barely audible.

Midas stiffened slightly, pulling back just enough to look at me. His eyes searched mine, filled with curiosity and a hint of unease. "Yes," he said softly. "Who did you draw?"

I hesitated for a second, the words stuck in my throat. But then I reached for the sketchpad, turning it around to show him what I had drawn.

His gaze dropped to the page, and I watched as his expression changed—from confusion to shock, and finally to something softer, more profound.

For a long moment, Midas simply stared at the sketch, his eyes tracing every line, every detail. I could see the realization dawning on him, the same recognition I had felt when I first saw those familiar eyes staring back at me from the page.

"We're having a girl?" he whispered, his voice thick with emotion. He looked up at me, his eyes wide and searching. "That's our little girl?"

I bit my lip, suddenly nervous, unsure of how he would react. "Yeah," I said softly, my voice trembling slightly. "That's our girl. Are you...are you sure you're ready for a girl? Girls are complicated and they'll paint your world pink."

Midas stared at me for a moment, and then, to my surprise, he smiled—a wide, genuine smile that lit up his entire face. "Cassidy, I don't care if we have a boy or a girl," he said, his voice filled with a warmth that made my heart swell. "She can paint the world whatever color she wants. I'm happy as long as they're ours. You and me, we've got this. Complicated or not, we can handle it."

I felt a wave of relief wash over me, my nerves easing as I looked into his eyes.

"I've been thinking about things, Cassidy. The team knows what they're doing. We don't have to be a part of every investigation. I want to make more time for living life. I need to do that. We need to do that. All of us."

He reached out, taking my hand in his, his touch gentle but firm. He helped me off the floor, and I set the sketchpad on the counter, letting it go for now.

We moved together, a silent understanding passing between us.

The weight of the night, the fear and tension that had held us both in its grip, began to melt away as we made our way to the bed. I could feel his love, his acceptance, wrapping around me like a blanket, and for the first time in a long time, I felt safe.

We fell into bed together, our bodies tangling as we sought comfort in each other's arms. The outside world, with all its darkness and terror, faded away as we lost ourselves in the moment, in the passion that had always connected us.

In that moment, there was no fear, no uncertainty—only us, and the life we were creating together.

The morning light was just beginning to filter through the curtains, casting a soft glow over the room. I woke slowly, my body still warm and content from the night before. Midas was still asleep beside me, his arm draped over my waist, his breath soft and even.

A faint rumble of hunger stirred in my stomach, reminding me that I hadn't eaten much the day before. Carefully, I slipped out of bed, trying not to wake him. I grabbed my robe from the chair and padded softly to the bathroom, intending to take a quick shower before finding something to eat.

But as I reached for the shower handle, my gaze fell on the sketchpad sitting on the counter. The events of the night before rushed back to me, and I felt a smile tug at the corners of my lips. I reached for the sketchpad, eager to look at the drawing again, to reconnect with the joy I had felt when I first realized who I had drawn.

But when I flipped open the cover, my heart nearly stopped.

The sketch—the beautiful, delicate sketch of our daughter—was ruined. Her face had been scratched out; the once-soft lines gouged harshly into the paper as if by an angry hand.

My pencil, the one I had used to create her image, lay beside the sketchpad, snapped clean in half.

*How did this happen? Who would do this?*

A cold wave of fear washed over me, freezing me in place. My mind raced, trying to make sense of what I was seeing, but there was no rational explanation.

I had left the sketch untouched the night before, and no one else had been in the bathroom. So how...how could this have happened?

Panic clawed at the edges of my mind, but before it could take hold, I heard Midas stirring in the bedroom. I hurriedly closed the sketchpad, my hands trembling as I shoved it under a pile of towels. I couldn't let him see this—not yet. Not until I understood what it meant.

Midas's voice, groggy with sleep, called out from the bedroom. "Cassidy? You in the shower?"

I forced myself to take a deep breath, pushing the fear down, burying it deep inside where it couldn't reach me. "Yeah," I called back, trying to keep my voice steady. "Just about to."

He appeared in the doorway, a lazy smile on his face as he rubbed the sleep from his eyes. "Mind if I join you?" he asked, his voice soft and teasing.

I hesitated for a split second, the image of the ruined sketch flashing in my mind. But then I looked at him—at the man I loved the father of my children—and I let the fear slip away.

Whatever had happened, whatever it meant, we would face it together. Just like we always did.

I smiled, stepping closer to him, my hands reaching for the hem of his shirt. "I'd like that," I whispered, letting myself get lost in the moment, letting him take me away from the darkness, if only for a little while.

As we stepped into the shower together, I let the warm water wash over me, carrying away the fear, the confusion, and the worry. There would be time to figure it all out later, but for now, I was content to lose myself in Midas's arms, to find solace in the love we shared.

But deep down, I knew that whatever had happened to that sketch, it was a sign.

A warning. And sooner or later, I would have to face it.

# Chapter Fourteen–Midas

The road stretched out before us, a dark ribbon cutting through the predawn stillness. The hum of the tires on the asphalt was the only sound, a low, steady drone that seemed to lull the SUV into a state of calm.

Inside, the atmosphere was heavy with exhaustion, each of us wrapped in our thoughts, replaying the events of the past few days like a movie on a loop.

I glanced around at my team, my family in every way that mattered. Macie was curled up in the backseat, her head resting against the window, eyes half-closed but still alert.

Sierra sat beside her, staring out into the night, lost in whatever thoughts were swirling in her mind. Jericho was behind the wheel, his hands gripping the steering wheel with a steadiness that belied the weariness etched into his face.

Cassidy sat beside me, her hand in mine, the warmth of her touch a reminder that we had made it through.

The exhaustion was bone-deep, a weight pressing down on my shoulders, but beneath it was something else—satisfaction. We had faced down an evil that had festered for over a century, and we had won. We had given those lost children a chance at peace, something that had been denied them for so long.

But even with that satisfaction, there was a lingering unease. I couldn't quite put my finger on it, but yeah, it was there.

The darkness we had confronted wasn't something that would just disappear. It was a part of our world, something we would always have to face, again and again. But for now, in this moment, there was a sense of accomplishment, of having done something truly good.

As the miles slipped by, I let myself relax, the tension slowly draining from my muscles. The quiet, the sense of finality, it was all a comfort.

We had done our job. We had made a difference.

The familiar sight of Gulf Coast Paranormal headquarters came into view as we turned the corner, the first light of dawn just beginning to paint the sky in soft hues of pink and orange.

The old, two-story building stood as a steadfast sentinel, welcoming us home after another mission was completed. My chest tightened with a mix of relief and pride as we pulled into the parking lot, the weight of the past few days easing just a little.

Jericho killed the engine, and for a moment, none of us moved.

The silence was thick, almost sacred, as we sat there, taking in the fact that we were back—together, safe, and whole. Finally, with a deep breath, I unbuckled my seatbelt and opened the door, the cool morning air hitting me like a refreshing slap to the face.

One by one, we climbed out of the SUV, the exhaustion still clinging to us, but there was something else now—a sense of camaraderie, of shared experience that had only strengthened our bond.

We had faced down horrors that would have broken lesser people, and yet here we were, standing tall.

As we began unloading the gear, I couldn't help but smile.

Each piece of equipment we hauled inside was a testament to the work we had done, to the lives we had touched and changed for the better. The nightmarish memories of the Tall Man, of the shadows and spirits that had tried to tear us apart, were already beginning to fade in the light of what we had accomplished.

I looked over at Cassidy as she hoisted a bag onto her shoulder, a determined set to her jaw despite the fatigue in her eyes.

My heart swelled with love and admiration for her. She was stronger than she gave herself credit for, and I knew that no matter what came next, we could face it together.

Inside, the headquarters was quiet, almost serene. The familiar scent of coffee and old books greeted us as we stepped through the door, and I felt a deep sense of relief wash over me.

This was our haven, our safe space where we could regroup and prepare for whatever came next. As I set down the last of the gear, I took a moment to let it all sink in.

We had made it. We had survived. And more than that, we had made a real difference in the world.

The darkness we fought was relentless, but so were we.

The creak of the old wooden floorboards echoed through the quiet of the headquarters as I made my way to my desk, the weight of exhaustion pulling at me with every step.

I could feel the adrenaline that had carried me through the past few days finally beginning to ebb, leaving behind a bone-deep weariness that threatened to pull me under.

I sank into the worn leather chair, letting out a long breath as I leaned back, closing my eyes for just a moment. The familiar surroundings were a comfort, a reminder that we were back in the world of the living, away from the darkness that had haunted us. But even as I tried to relax, the tension in my shoulders refused to ease completely.

My hand drifted to the stack of files Sierra had left on my desk. I hadn't pressed her for details. There would be time to talk later, time to figure out which case was next. For now, all I wanted was a moment of peace, a brief respite from the chaos.

But the universe had other plans.

The sharp ring of the phone cut through the silence, startling me out of my thoughts. I hesitated, my hand hovering over the receiver as a sense of dread settled in my gut.

I knew that call. That particular ring always signaled something urgent, something that couldn't wait.

For a brief moment, I considered letting it go to voicemail. Just a few more minutes of quiet, a few more moments to catch my breath. But I knew I couldn't. This was the life we had chosen, the responsibility we had taken on, and it didn't wait for anyone.

With a sigh, I picked up the receiver, bracing myself for whatever was about to come.

"Gulf Coast Paranormal, this is Midas."

The voice on the other end was trembling, filled with anxiety and desperation. "Is this...is this Midas Demopolis? The paranormal investigator?"

"Yes, it is," I replied, my voice calm and steady, despite the knot tightening in my stomach. "How can I help you?"

The person on the other end let out a shaky breath, and I could almost feel the weight of their fear through the phone. "I need your help...please. It's my daughter. She...she's been seeing things. Dark things. We just bought the Malaga Inn in Mobile. I think...I think something is after her."

The familiar thrill of anticipation shot through me, mingled with exhaustion, I couldn't quite shake.

I jotted down the details on a notepad, my mind already shifting gears, readying itself for the next case. The work was never done, and as much as I wanted to rest, I knew I couldn't turn away someone in need.

"The Malaga Inn?" I asked, keeping my voice steady and reassuring as I continued to take notes. "I've driven by there a few times. Tell me more."

I leaned back in my chair, a small smile tugging at the corners of my lips despite the fatigue pulling at me.

Another mystery, another chance to help someone find peace. The darkness was relentless, but so were we.

I finished scribbling the last few details on the notepad, my mind already working through the logistics of the new case.

Mobile was home base for us but something told me this one wouldn't be easy either. They never were. But that was okay—this was what we did. This was who we were.

*Look at me. Already resisting taking a break.*

As I hung up the phone, a small smile spread across my face. There was always another mystery waiting, another family in need of our help. The thrill of the chase, the challenge of uncovering the truth—it was in my blood, a part of me I couldn't deny.

But as I looked around the quiet headquarters, at the weary faces of my team as they moved about, unpacking the last of the gear, I knew we couldn't jump right back into the fray.

Not yet. We needed time to recover, to regroup. And more than that, I needed time with Cassidy. Time to be with her, to celebrate the life we were building together.

I had a surprise planned, something to remind Cassidy that no matter how dark our work got, there was always light in our lives. I couldn't wait to see the look on her face when I showed her. I'd let the team rest, let them enjoy a brief moment of peace before the next storm rolled in.

We'd earned it.

I leaned back in my chair, letting the exhaustion wash over me for just a moment. The next adventure was calling, but for the first time in a long while, I was going to make sure we took a break before diving in.

Because no matter how much the darkness tried to pull us under, we always had each other.

And that was enough.

# Epilogue–Cassidy

The soft glow of the afternoon sun filtered through the windows of my art studio, casting a warm, golden hue over everything. The familiar scent of pencils, paper, and paint filled the air, grounding me in this peaceful space where I could lose myself in my work. I sat at my desk, my sketchbook open before me, the paper still fresh and crisp under my fingers.

With each stroke of my pencil, the image of Dead Children's Playground came to life on the page, but this time, it was different.

The shadows that once clung to the edges of the playground were gone, replaced by a gentle, golden light that bathed everything in warmth. The swings, which had once creaked eerily in the darkness, now swayed softly in the breeze, their movement calm and rhythmic.

I drew the children next, their forms ethereal but full of life, their faces lit up with joy as they played.

Their spirits, once trapped in fear and darkness, were now free, released from the torment that had held them captive for so long.

The playground, which had been a place of nightmares, was now a sanctuary, a place where the children could finally find peace.

As I added the final touches, the last hints of sunlight dancing across the page, I felt a profound sense of closure wash over me. This was the way it was meant to be. The spirits of the children were no longer bound by the past, but were free to move on, to play and laugh as they were meant to.

I could almost hear their laughter, soft and sweet, carried on the breeze.

I couldn't help but smile as I shaded the last few details, my heart swelling with a mixture of relief and satisfaction. This case had been different, more personal somehow.

The weight of what we had done, of the lives we had touched, lingered in my mind, a reminder of why we did this work.

It wasn't just about chasing shadows or documenting the supernatural; it was about helping those who couldn't help themselves, about giving a voice to the silenced, and bringing peace to those who had been denied it for too long.

As I worked, I reflected on the journey we'd been on. It had been harrowing, filled with moments of terror and doubt, but it had also been meaningful. We had faced down something truly dark and dangerous, and we had come out the other side stronger for it.

The children, those lost souls who had suffered so much, were finally at rest, and that was something worth celebrating.

This sketch, this image of the playground bathed in light, was my way of honoring them, of acknowledging the battle we had fought and the peace we had won.

It was a testament to the resilience of the human spirit, to the idea that even in the darkest of places, light could still find a way to shine through.

I set down my pencil, my gaze lingering on the finished sketch. The image was complete, the playground was now a place of light and life rather than fear and darkness.

My heart was full, the emotions of the past few days still raw but also tempered by the knowledge that we had made a difference.

This journey, as difficult as it had been, had reaffirmed my belief in the mission of Gulf Coast Paranormal.

Our work was more than just investigating the unexplained; it was about giving a voice to those who had been forgotten, about bringing peace to those who had been restless for too long.

It was about shining a light into the darkest corners of the world and saying, "You are not alone. We are here, and we will help you."

The children's spirits were free now, their laughter no longer tainted by fear, their souls no longer trapped in a place of torment. And that was worth everything.

I carefully closed the sketchbook, running my fingers over the cover as a deep sense of contentment settled over me. This case had been one of the most challenging we had faced, but it had also been one of the most rewarding. Certainly in comparison to the loss of Jocelyn Graves but we almost lost someone else though. My hand went to my belly.

We had fought hard, we had struggled, and we had won. The children's spirits were finally at rest, and that was something I would carry with me always.

But I also knew that this wasn't the end.

There would be more challenges ahead, more darkness to face, and more spirits in need of help. And I was ready. We were ready. The team I was a part of was strong, and resilient, and together, we could handle anything that came our way.

Midas might say he was taking time off but I knew better. We needed to take a break once in a while but quit?

Never.

As I sat there, the studio quiet around me, I felt a deep sense of peace. We had done something truly good, something that mattered. And that was enough.

But as the sense of peace began to settle in, a shadow of doubt crept in.

My mind drifted back to the sketch I had made the night before, the image of our daughter, her face scratched out in a way that had sent a chill down my spine. I hadn't told Midas about it, hadn't wanted to worry him, but the image haunted me.

What did it mean? Was it just a manifestation of my fears, or was it something more?

I pushed the thoughts away, determined not to let them take root. There was no sense in worrying Midas, not when there was so much to be grateful for, so much to look forward to.

However, the worry lingered at the back of my mind, a reminder that even when standing in the light, shadows could still find a way to creep in.

I stood up from the desk and walked over to the mirror, my hand resting gently on my small baby bump.

I could feel her there, growing, a new life full of potential and promise. A future that was ours to protect.

"I'll keep you safe," I whispered, my voice soft but filled with determination. "I promise."

And as I stood there, gazing at my reflection, I felt a renewed sense of purpose. There would be more battles to fight, more darkness to face, but I would face it all, for her, for our family, and for the team that had become my second family.

No matter what came our way, I would be ready.

We would all be ready.

# Author's Note

As I bring this installment of the Gulf Coast Paranormal series to a close, I want to extend my heartfelt thanks to each and every reader who has journeyed with me into the eerie and mysterious world of the paranormal.

Writing *Dead Children's Playground* was both a thrilling and chilling experience, and it reminded me of the power of storytelling in exploring the unknown and the unexplained.

The haunted playground in Huntsville, Alabama, is a real place with a history that has intrigued and unsettled locals for generations. It serves as a powerful reminder that some places are steeped in mystery and hold on to their secrets tightly. My hope is that this story captured the essence of those mysteries and conveyed the deep sense of unease that such locations can inspire. My story is a bit of fiction. There is no Tall Man stalking the Maple Hill Cemetery or the playground.

But I am constantly inspired by the world of the supernatural and the questions it raises about life, death, and what might lie beyond. It is my goal to bring those stories to life in a way that both entertains and provokes thought.

I made a personal trip to this beautiful place. If you get the chance to stop in Huntsville, be sure and visit the playground. Say hello to any spirits you encounter. To my loyal readers, I am deeply grateful for your continued support of my writing. Your enthusiasm for the Gulf Coast Paranormal series drives me to dive deeper into the unknown and to continue crafting stories that keep you on the edge of your seat.

There's more to come, the details of which I'll be sure and share with you as soon as I can. If this book sent a shiver down your spine or made you question what might be lurking in the shadows, then I consider my job well done.

Stay tuned for more adventures, more hauntings, and more mysteries as we continue to explore the darkest corners of the paranormal world.

Thank you for being part of this journey. Please, follow me on Facebook[1] or email me. Visit my website if you'd like a signed paperback of any of my books. Just go to MLBullock.com[2].

Until next time, keep your eyes open and your heart brave.

Warmest regards,

M. L. Bullock

---

1. https://www.facebook.com/AuthorMLBullock

2. https://www.mlbullock.com/

# M. L. Bullock's Book List

If you think you've missed one of my books, here is a comprehensive list of everything. All books are available on Amazon Kindle, and as paper books. Some are available as audiobooks.

SEVEN SISTERS

#1 Seven Sisters[1]

#2 Moonlight Falls on Seven Sisters[2]

#3 Shadows Stir at Seven Sisters[3]

#4 The Stars That Fell[4]

#5 The Stars We Walked Upon[5]

#6 The Sun Rises Over Seven Sisters[6]

#7 Beyond Seven Sisters[7]

Bonus Christmas at Seven Sisters[8]

Bonus The Ghost on the Swing[9]

#8 Silent Night, Haunted Night[10]

#9 Haunted Halls of Rosegate Manor[11]

#10 Terror at Mossy Oak[12]

---


1. https://www.amazon.com/Seven-Sisters-Book-ebook/dp/B00MQ994T6

2. https://www.amazon.com/gp/product/B00PR3014K

3. https://www.amazon.com/gp/product/B00V2QOYYO

4. https://www.amazon.com/gp/product/B016FWP7FY

5. https://www.amazon.com/gp/product/B01BN8F76O

6. https://www.amazon.com/gp/product/B01GFBR9HY

7. https://www.amazon.com/gp/product/B08RWB61KV

8. https://www.amazon.com/Christmas-Seven-Sisters-M-L-Bullock-ebook/dp/B0768Q7371

9. https://www.amazon.com/Ghost-Swing-Seven-Sisters-Book-ebook/dp/B07G66LS9D

10. https://www.amazon.com/Silent-Night-Haunted-Seven-Sisters-ebook/dp/B0CQ6YTQD8

11. https://www.amazon.com/Haunted-Halls-Rosegate-Sisters-Mystery-ebook/dp/B0CGXWXT3P

#11 Dark Angel of Selma[13]

#11 Ghost of the Tangled Garden

#12 Fear at the Foxglove Inn

#13 The Shadow Staircase

The Ultimate Seven Sisters Collection[14]

Seven Sisters Collection Vol. 1[15]

Seven Sisters Collection Vol. 2[16]

Seven Sisters Collection Vol. 3[17]

IDLEWOOD

#1 The Ghosts of Idlewood[18]

#2 Dreams of Idlewood[19]

#3 The Whispering Saint[20]

#4 The Haunted Child[21]

The Hauntings of Idlewood[22]

RETURN TO SEVEN SISTERS

#1 The Roses of Mobile[23]

#2 All the Summer Roses[24]

---


12.     https://www.amazon.com/gp/product/B0CVMD1GPB

13.     https://www.amazon.com/Dark-Angel-Selma-Seven-Sisters-ebook/dp/B0CXPLYWMT

14.     https://www.amazon.com/Ultimate-Seven-Sisters-Collection-ebook/dp/B01J8HUWI0

15.     https://www.amazon.com/Seven-Sisters-Collection-M-Bullock-ebook/dp/
B0CR1R77KB

16.     https://www.amazon.com/gp/product/B0CR1VHL9L

17.     https://www.amazon.com/Seven-Sisters-Collection-M-Bullock-ebook/dp/
B0CYCWLG5W

18.     https://www.amazon.com/Ghosts-Idlewood-M-L-Bullock-ebook/dp/B01M0Q8JGS

19.     https://www.amazon.com/gp/product/B01M9DPIBL

20.     https://www.amazon.com/gp/product/B01MZ7BNE8

21.     https://www.amazon.com/gp/product/B06Y14W67X

22.     https://www.amazon.com/Hauntings-Idlewood-M-L-Bullock-ebook/dp/B09JRX7G5B

23.     https://www.amazon.com/Roses-Mobile-Return-Seven-Sisters-ebook/dp/B07175TFYH

24.     https://www.amazon.com/gp/product/B075WM7CYR

#3 Blooms Torn Asunder[25]

#4 A Garden of Thorns[26]

#5 Wreath of Roses[27]

<u>Return to Seven Sisters Collection</u>[28]

THE GRACEFIELD HAUNTINGS

#1 Haunted Gracefield[29]

#2 The Three Graces[30]

#3 Grace Before Dying[31]

<u>The Gracefield Hauntings Collection</u>[32]

MARIETTA

#1 The Bones of Marietta[33]

#2 Footsteps of Angels[34]

THE BEAUMONT SAGA: A SEVEN SISTERS PREQUEL

#1 Olivia[35]

#2 Louis[36]

#3 Christine[37]

---


25. https://www.amazon.com/gp/product/B0793NKTVM

26. https://www.amazon.com/gp/product/B07F6FGKT4

27. https://www.amazon.com/gp/product/B07L3BRK7B

28. https://www.amazon.com/Return-Seven-Sisters-M-L-Bullock-ebook/dp/B07RB7LBW2

29. https://www.amazon.com/Haunted-Gracefield-Hauntings-Book-ebook/dp/
B07RYB89NF

30. https://www.amazon.com/gp/product/B07X7J5NKC

31. https://www.amazon.com/gp/product/B089G9BZVM

32. https://www.amazon.com/Gracefield-Hauntings-Complete-Collection-ebook/dp/
B08DN9DNZ9

33. https://www.amazon.com/Bones-Marietta-M-L-Bullock-ebook/dp/B08LQVFHP8

34. https://www.amazon.com/gp/product/B098XVTJQR

35. https://www.amazon.com/Olivia-Seven-Sisters-Prequel-Beaumont-ebook/dp/
B09MV956KT

36. https://www.amazon.com/Louis-Beaumont-Saga-Book-2-ebook/dp/B0B53ZWWT5

37. https://www.amazon.com/gp/product/B0BR472H4X

<u>The Beaumont Saga</u>[38]
DEVECHEAUX ANTIQUES AND HAUNTED THINGS
#1 A Cup of Shadows[39]
#2 A Voice From Her Past[40]
#3 A Watch of Weeping Angels[41]
#4 The Ghost Mirror[42]
#5 The Phantom Lamp[43]
#6 The Darkening Door[44]
#7 Kalliope's Dollhouse[45]
#8 The Mourning Heart (2024)
<u>Devecheaux Antiques and Haunted Things Trilogy Volume 1</u>[46]
<u>Devecheaux Antiques and Haunted Things Trilogy Volume 2</u>[47]
SUGAR HILL
#1 Wife of the Left Hand[48]
#2 Fire on the Ramparts[49]
#3 Blood By Candlelight[50]

---


38.     https://www.amazon.com/dp/B0C19Q6VTQ

39.     https://www.amazon.com/Shadows-Devecheaux-Antiques-Haunted-Things-ebook/dp/B08GH5DFVX

40.     https://www.amazon.com/gp/product/B08KK9C8SJ

41.     https://www.amazon.com/gp/product/B08PQGLTDG

42.     https://www.amazon.com/gp/product/B09GLCFX84

43.     https://www.amazon.com/dp/B09S7MCPMG

44.     https://www.amazon.com/Darkening-Devecheaux-Antiques-Haunted-Things-ebook/dp/B0BLTJT9GP

45.     https://www.amazon.com/Kalliopes-Dollhouse-Devecheaux-Antiques-Haunted-ebook/dp/B0BWZHFGG8

46.     https://www.amazon.com/Devecheaux-Antiques-Haunted-Things-Trilogy-ebook/dp/B09DQVDMVN

47.     https://www.amazon.com/dp/B0C1BD6BJ5

48.     https://www.amazon.com/Wife-Left-Hand-Sugar-Hill-ebook/dp/B01M0XJ032

49.     https://www.amazon.com/gp/product/B01MSYQA1L

#4 The Starlight Ball[51]

#5 His Lovely Garden[52]

<u>The Sugar Hill Collection</u>[53]

THE GHOSTS OF SUMMERLEIGH

#1 The Belles of Desire, Mississippi[54]

#2 The Ghost of Jeopardy Belle[55]

#3 The Lady in White[56]

#4 Loxley Belle[57]

<u>The Ghosts of Summerleigh</u>[58]

SOUTHERN GOTHIC SERIES

#1 Being With Beau[59]

#2 Death's Last Darling[60]

#3 Spook House[61]

The Southern Gothic Collection

WELCOME TO DEAD HOUSE

#1 Never Dead[62]

---


50. https://www.amazon.com/gp/product/B01NA0NL8U

51. https://www.amazon.com/gp/product/B071KYVMYF

52. https://www.amazon.com/gp/product/B078WFHYNM

53. https://www.amazon.com/Sugar-Hill-Collection-M-L-Bullock-ebook/dp/B074JD4SPN

54. https://www.amazon.com/Belles-Desire-Mississippi-Ghosts-Summerleigh-ebook/dp/B0778QS6CW

55. https://www.amazon.com/gp/product/B079SM3CK

56. https://www.amazon.com/gp/product/B07CRLFV4Z

57. https://www.amazon.com/gp/product/B07Q14NCQX

58. https://www.amazon.com/Ghosts-Summerleigh-Collection-M-L-Bullock-ebook/dp/B07FNCYFTP

59. https://www.amazon.com/Being-Beau-Southern-Gothic-Book-ebook/dp/B07MXS8FVX

60. https://www.amazon.com/gp/product/B07SBP3XRZ

61. https://www.amazon.com/gp/product/B08GN6ZJG7

62. https://www.amazon.com/Never-Dead-Welcome-House-Book-ebook/dp/B086BBNSFG

#2 Always Dead[63]

#3 Dead at Midnight[64]

<u>Welcome to Dead House Series</u>[65]

HAUNTING PASSIONS

#1 For the Love of Shadows[66]

#2 Her Haunted Heart[67]

<u>Haunting Passions</u>[68]

GULF COAST PARANORMAL Season One

#1 The Ghosts of Kali Oka Road[69]

#2 The Ghosts of the Crescent Theater[70]

#3 A Haunting on Bloodgood Row[71]

#4 The Legend of the Ghost Queen[72]

#5 A Haunting at Dixie House[73]

#6 The Ghost Lights of Forrest Field[74]

#7 The Ghost of Gabrielle Bonet[75]

---


63.    https://www.amazon.com/gp/product/B088TS6CRW

64.    https://www.amazon.com/gp/product/B08BJ78VQC

65.    https://www.amazon.com/Welcome-Dead-House-Complete-Boxed-ebook/dp/B08Q3KMHW2

66.    https://www.amazon.com/Love-Shadows-Haunting-Passions-Book-ebook/dp/B07YQMFVPY

67.    https://www.amazon.com/Haunted-Heart-Haunting-Passions-Book-ebook/dp/B09MTQZPDC

68.    https://www.amazon.com/dp/B0B359YMK5

69.    https://www.amazon.com/Ghosts-Kali-Road-Coast-Paranormal-ebook/dp/B01MT5P7XY

70.    https://www.amazon.com/gp/product/B06XJRZNTX

71.    https://www.amazon.com/gp/product/B06Y175VSZ

72.    https://www.amazon.com/gp/product/B07237WVBF

73.    https://www.amazon.com/gp/product/B074VB73Z2

74.    https://www.amazon.com/gp/product/B075JKJD9F?

75.    https://www.amazon.com/gp/product/B077H1FRW7

#8 The Ghost of Harrington Farm[76]

#9 The Creature on Crenshaw Road[77]

#10 A Ghostly Ride in Gulfport[78]

#11 The Maelstrom of the Leaf Academy[79]

#12 The Ghosts of Phoenix No 7[80]

#13 The Ghosts of Oakleigh House[81]

#14 The Spirits of Brady Hall[82]

#15 The Gray Lady of Wilmer[83]

Bonus The October People[84] (A Gulf Coast Paranormal Extra)

GULF COAST PARANORMAL TRILOGY

#1 Ghosted[85]

#2 Haunted[86]

#3 Spooked[87]

#4 Dead[88]

#5 Paranormal[89]

<u>#6 Delta Hex</u>

---


76. https://www.amazon.com/gp/product/B079V8ZNDF

77. https://www.amazon.com/gp/product/B07D44SYPB

78. https://www.amazon.com/gp/product/B07GDWV2CC

79. https://www.amazon.com/gp/product/B07NGMV839

80. https://www.amazon.com/gp/product/B07RYB98VW

81. https://www.amazon.com/gp/product/B07V25DKW7

82. https://www.amazon.com/gp/product/B07ZMHZ7YL

83. https://www.amazon.com/gp/product/B083QQ16FG

84. https://www.amazon.com/October-People-Coast-Paranormal-Extra-ebook/dp/
B07JLNCCGK

85. https://www.amazon.com/Ghosted-Gulf-Coast-Paranormal-Trilogy-ebook/dp/
B096MWTXXS

86. https://www.amazon.com/gp/product/B096MX95J1

87. https://www.amazon.com/gp/product/B096SR47KV

88. https://www.amazon.com/gp/product/B096T6XLS8

89. https://www.amazon.com/gp/product/B096TK52QK

#7 Delta Dead

#8 Shadowed

<u>Gulf Coast Paranormal Season One Boxed Set</u>[90]

Gulf Coast Paranormal Season Two Boxed Set

GULF COAST PARANORMAL SEASON TWO

#1 The Wayland Manor Haunting[91]

#2 The Beast of Limerick House[92]

#3 The Haunting at Goliath Cave[93]

#4 The Skeleton's Key[94]

#5 Death Among the Roses[95]

#6 The Spiritus Mirror[96]

#7 The Captain of Water Street[97]

#8 Return to the Leaf Academy[98]

#9 The Rising of Lucy Vallow[99]

Bonus Horror Ever After[100] (A Gulf Coast Paranormal Extra)

GULF COAST PARANORMAL SEASON THREE

---


90.    https://www.amazon.com/Gulf-Coast-Paranormal-Season-One-ebook/dp/ B08JD3PNZB

91.    https://www.amazon.com/Wayland-Manor-Haunting-Paranormal-Season-ebook/dp/ B08LQRP5V1

92.    https://www.amazon.com/gp/product/B08ZHYNDVX?

93.    https://www.amazon.com/gp/product/B09DP1LZXX

94.    https://www.amazon.com/Skeletons-Gulf-Coast-Paranormal-Season-ebook/dp/ B09PC7R1QJ

95.    https://www.amazon.com/Death-Among-Roses-Paranormal-Season-ebook/dp/ B09YFZ1Q4H/

96.    https://www.amazon.com/gp/product/B0B9NZDB6X

97.    https://www.amazon.com/dp/B0C17S9YXK

98.    https://www.amazon.com/dp/B0CCB37NPW

99.    https://www.amazon.com/Rising-Vallow-Coast-Paranormal-Season-ebook/dp/ B0C17W7VTR

100.    https://www.amazon.com/gp/product/B09DP1FVXP

#1 Tower of Darkness[101]

#2 Haunted Molly[102]

#3 Dead Children's Playground[103]

#4 The Malaga Demon

#5 Haunting at Barton Academy

#6 The Outlaw Screamer

TWELVE TO MIDNIGHT

#1 Mary Twelves[104]

#2 Pieces of Twelves[105]

BRYNN LEEDS HAUNTING

#1 We Walk in Darkness[106]

MORGAN'S ROCK

#1 The Haunting of Joanna Storm[107]

#2 The Hall of Shadows[108]

#3 The Ghost of Joanna Storm[109]

The Haunting at Morgan's Rock Trilogy[110]

QUEEN MUMMY

#1 Queen Mummy[111]


101.    https://www.amazon.com/Tower-Darkness-Coast-Paranormal-Season-ebook/dp/B0CQGVCV2S

102.    https://www.amazon.com/gp/product/B0CQGT95SG

103.    https://www.amazon.com/Childrens-Playground-Coast-Paranormal-Season-ebook/dp/B0D6TS6LS2

104.    https://www.amazon.com/Mary-Twelves-M-L-Bullock-ebook/dp/B08LQVMCRY

105.    https://www.amazon.com/dp/B0BR8GD3T2

106.    https://www.amazon.com/Darkness-Brynn-Leeds-Haunting-Novel-ebook/dp/B08PP4X561

107.    https://www.amazon.com/Haunting-Joanna-Storm-Morgans-Rock-ebook/dp/B07KQHBLMV

108.    https://www.amazon.com/gp/product/B07LFK2QR7

109.    https://www.amazon.com/gp/product/B07ND55PBL

110.    https://www.amazon.com/Haunting-at-Morgans-Rock-ebook/dp/B07TKMLFJR

RIVER RUN
#1 River Run[112]
#2 Blood Run[113]
#3 Witch Child[114]
River Run Collection
SOUTHLAND
#1 Southland[115]
#2 Southland: Legacy[116]
#3 Southland: Reborn (2024)
Southland: The Complete Collection
THE DESERT QUEEN
#1 The Tale of Nefret[117]
#2 The Falcon Rises[118]
#3 The Kingdom of Nefertiti[119]
#4 The Song of the Bee Eater[120]
The Desert Queen Collection[121]
LOST CAMELOT
#1 Guinevere Forever[122]
#2 Guinevere Unconquered[123]

---


111.    https://www.amazon.com/Queen-Mummy-Queens-Revenge-Book-ebook/dp/ B0B8F4QDP9

112.    https://www.amazon.com/River-Run-M-L-Bullock-ebook/dp/B0BQ9WVKPJ

113.    https://www.amazon.com/Blood-Run-River-Book-ebook/dp/B0CGXZ5GWW

114.    https://www.amazon.com/Witch-Child-River-Run-Book-ebook/dp/B0CSR1PKVV/

115.    https://www.amazon.com/Southland-M-L-Bullock-ebook/dp/B0BWPVJ2XP

116.    https://www.amazon.com/Southland-Legacy-M-L-Bullock-ebook/dp/B0CJH32K6D

117.    https://www.amazon.com/Tale-Nefret-Desert-Queen-Saga-ebook/dp/B08WRKKV88

118.    https://www.amazon.com/gp/product/B08WWQLB8Q

119.    https://www.amazon.com/gp/product/B08WR5YX3D

120.    https://www.amazon.com/gp/product/B08WWJDJHL

121.    https://www.amazon.com/Desert-Queen-Collection-M-L-Bullock-ebook/dp/ B01MRU3GLH

#3 The Undead Queen of Camelot[124]
Lost Camelot Trilogy[125]
SHABBY HEARTS (A Romantic Comedy Series)
#1 A Touch of Shabby[126]
#2 Shabbier By the Minute[127]
#3 Shabby By Night[128]
#4 Shabby All the Way[129]
#5 Star Spangled Shabby[130]
#6 A Shabby Wedding (Coming in 2024)
MISCELLANEOUS
Ghosts on a Plane[131]
Dead Is the Loneliest Place to Be[132]
After Ella[133]
Ghosts of the Atlantis[134]
BY MONICA BULLOCK
Delivered Me From Evil[135]

---


122.     https://www.amazon.com/Guinevere-Forever-Lost-Camelot-Book-ebook/dp/ B0764J39GC

123.     https://www.amazon.com/gp/product/B0786ZKBND

124.     https://www.amazon.com/gp/product/B07PFFCYQ5

125.     https://www.amazon.com/Lost-Camelot-Trilogy-Book-ebook/dp/B07R7XBFV2

126.     https://www.amazon.com/Touch-Shabby-Hearts-Paranormal-Mystery-ebook/dp/ B07CTD7M95

127.     https://www.amazon.com/gp/product/B07DCD3WW6

128.     https://www.amazon.com/gp/product/B07DCDSWKN

129.     https://www.amazon.com/gp/product/B07KYDK7YP

130.     https://www.amazon.com/gp/product/B084HN9T9Z

131.     https://www.amazon.com/Ghosts-Plane-M-L-Bullock-ebook/dp/B0713YWSCJ

132.     https://www.amazon.com/Dead-Loneliest-Place-Be-Bullock-ebook/dp/B0BGV9PP3T

133.     https://www.amazon.com/After-Ella-M-L-Bullock-ebook/dp/B0C6GCLR24

134.     https://www.amazon.com/Ghosts-Atlantis-M-L-Bullock-ebook/dp/B0CC152F89

135.    https://www.amazon.com/Delivered-Me-Evil-Deliverance-Supernatural-ebook/dp/
B08KRNPLB3

# Don't miss out!

Visit the website below and you can sign up to receive emails whenever M.L. Bullock publishes a new book. There's no charge and no obligation.

https://books2read.com/r/B-A-CXMC-CMNUE

BOOKS 2 READ

Connecting independent readers to independent writers.

# Also by M.L. Bullock

**Create and Prosper**
The Prolific Writer: How to Write and Create a Successful Catalog of Books

**Desert Queen Saga**
The Tale of Nefret
The Falcon Rises
The Kingdom of Nefertiti
The Song of the Bee Eater

**Devecheaux Antiques and Haunted Things Trilogy Series**
Devecheaux Antiques and Haunted Things
A Cup of Shadows
A Voice From Her Past
A Watch Of Weeping Angels

**Gulf Coast Paranormal**
The Ghosts of Kali Oka Road

The Ghosts of the Crescent Theater
A Haunting on Bloodgood Row
The Legend of the Ghost Queen
A Haunting at Dixie House
The Ghost Lights of Forrest Field
The Ghost of Gabrielle Bonet
The Ghost of Harrington Farm
The Creature on Crenshaw Road
A Ghostly Ride in Gulfport
The Ghosts of Phoenix No.7
The Maelstrom of the Leaf Academy
The Ghosts of Oakleigh House
The Spirits of Brady Hall
The Gray Lady of Wilmer


**Gulf Coast Paranormal Season Three**
Tower of Darkness
Haunted Molly
Dead Children's Playground


**Gulf Coast Paranormal Season Two**
The Wayland Manor Haunting
The Beast of Limerick House
The Beast of Limerick House
A Haunting at Goliath Cave
Death Among the Roses
The Captain of Water Street
Return to the Leaf Academy

**Gulf Coast Paranormal Trilogy Series**
Ghosted
Haunted
Dead
Spooked
Paranormal


**Haunting Passions**
For the Love of Shadows
Her Haunted Heart


**Idlewood**
The Ghosts of Idlewood
Dreams of Idlewood
The Whispering Saint
The Haunted Child


**Laurel House**
Whispers


**Lost Camelot**
Guinevere Unconquered
The Undead Queen of Camelot

**Lost Camelot Trilogy**
Guinevere Forever


**Marietta**
The Bones of Marietta
Footsteps of Angels


**Morgans Rock**
The Haunting of Joanna Storm
The Hall of Shadows
The Ghost of Joanna Storm


**Return to Seven Sisters**
The Roses of Mobile
All the Summer Roses
Blooms Torn Asunder
A Garden of Thorns
Wreath of Roses


**River Run**
River Run


**Scary Fall Stories**

Horrible Little Things


**Seven Sisters**
Seven Sisters
Moonlight Falls On Seven Sisters
Shadows Stir At Seven Sisters
The Stars That Fell
The Stars We Walked Upon
The Sun Rises Over Seven Sisters
Beyond Seven Sister
Ghost on a Swing


**Shabby Hearts**
A Touch Of Shabby
Shabbier By The Minute
Shabby By Night
Shabby All The Way
Star Spangled Shabby


**Southern Gothic**
Being With Beau
Death's Last Darling
Spook House


**Southland**
Southland

**Sugar Hill**
Wife Of The Left Hand
Fire On The Ramparts
Blood By Candlelight
The Starlight Ball
His Lovely Garden


**Summerleigh**
The Belles of Desire, Mississippi
The Ghost Of Jeoprady Belle
The Lady In White
Loxley Belle


**Supernatural Support Group**
Circle of Shadows


**The Mummy Queen's Revenge**
Queen Mummy


**Twelve to Midnight**
Mary Twelves


**Standalone**

The Hauntings of Idlewood
Lost Camelot
The Desert Queen Collection
Haunting Passions
Ghosts on a Plane
Halloween Screams
Dead Is the Loneliest Place to Be
Ghost Story
Believer's Guide to Paranormal Ministry
Haunted Chronicles of the Leaf Academy


Watch for more at www.mlbullock.com.

# About the Author

Author M.L. Bullock enjoys the laid-back atmosphere and the spooky vibe of the Gulf Coast, especially the region's historic districts and sites. When she isn't visiting her favorite haunts in New Orleans or Old Mobile, you can find her flipping through old photographs or newspaper clippings in search of new inspiration.

Read more at www.mlbullock.com.

www.ingramcontent.com/pod-product-compliance
Lightning Source LLC
Chambersburg PA
CBHW060925140726
47996CB00001B/391